"Hi, Porter!"

"Lily—"

She blinked. "Your voice sounds odd. Are you all right?"

"I am now that I know you are."

Lily gripped her phone tighter. "What do you mean?"

"Sheriff Granger is on speakerphone with me. Are your parents there?"

"Yes?" She couldn't imagine what was going on.

"He wants to have a five-way conversation."

A chill ran down her body. "All right. They're in the kitchen. I'll go in and put my phone on speaker." She hurried back to the kitchen and looked at her parents. "Porter is with the sheriff. He wants to talk to all of us."

Perplexed, her parents gathered around the phone. "We're listening, Sheriff."

"Mr. and Mrs. Owens? Ms. Owens? This is Sheriff Granger. Ranger Ewing is here in my office with me. We've arrested the culprit that Ranger Ewing tangled with in the mountains recently. Tonight a lot more information has come forth."

Lily started to tremble.

Dear Reader,

Tragedy or destiny?

I've often thought about the triumph of the human spirit. How often do we hear or read about a person who has met with a horrible tragedy? We think how unfair it is. How terrible. We ask ourselves how he or she survived.

Then we find out they not only survived, they *thrived*!

I wrote this book, *Home on the Ranch: Wyoming Cowboy Ranger*, to celebrate the story of a woman whose life started out on one path, but because of a tragedy, she had to call on her courage to turn her whole life around in a brand-new way. In the process she not only helped herself, she made the world a better place for everyone around her and found love.

I adore stories of people who not only survived, they conquered! I hope you do, too.

Enjoy!

Rebecca Winters

HOME *on the* RANCH

WYOMING COWBOY RANGER

✤

REBECCA WINTERS

HARLEQUIN® HOME ON THE RANCH

Recycling programs
for this product may
not exist in your area.

ISBN-13: 978-1-335-83489-8
ISBN-13: 978-1-335-04188-3 (Direct to Consumer edition)

Home on the Ranch: Wyoming Cowboy Ranger

Printed in U.S.A.

Rebecca Winters, whose family of four children has now swelled to include five beautiful grandchildren, lives in Salt Lake City, Utah, in the land of the Rocky Mountains. Living near canyons and high alpine meadows full of wildflowers, she never runs out of places to explore. They, plus her favorite vacation spots in Europe, often end up as backgrounds for her romance novels, because writing is her passion, along with her family and church.

Rebecca loves to hear from readers. If you wish to email her, please visit her website, rebeccawinters.net.

Books by Rebecca Winters

Harlequin Western Romance

Wind River Cowboys

The Right Cowboy
Stranded with the Rancher
Home on the Ranch: Wyoming Sheriff

Sapphire Mountain Cowboys

A Valentine for the Cowboy
Made for the Rancher
Cowboy Doctor
Roping Her Christmas Cowboy

Lone Star Lawmen

The Texas Ranger's Bride
The Texas Ranger's Nanny
The Texas Ranger's Family
Her Texas Ranger Hero

Visit the Author Profile page
at Harlequin.com for more titles.

To every survivor, whoever you are,
who faced tragedy and turned it into triumph.
You've helped all of us find hope and a reason
to believe in the power of the human spirit.

Chapter 1

Whitebark, Wyoming

Lily Owens hurried into the physiotherapy clinic at Whitebark Hospital, where she'd been working for the last three months. She hated to be late for work, but one of the mares on her parents' ranch had gone into labor and she'd stayed to help until the vet arrived.

"Hi, Lily! Mr. Harrington is in the examining room."

"Thanks, Cindy. Any messages?"

"Not yet," the receptionist responded.

Lily went down the hall to the closet for her white lab coat. She slipped it on over her short-sleeved yellow top and cropped white jeans. On the way to her office, she passed the recently divorced head of the physio-therapy clinic, Dr. Matt Jensen, who was already busy at work. He stopped to talk to her before going into another examining room.

"I'm glad I caught you before the day got away from us. How would you like to join me for dinner and a movie next Friday?"

Caught was right. Matt was nice-looking and friendly, but she wasn't attracted to him and needed to think fast. "Matt? I'm flattered that you would ask me out, but I don't think it's a good idea since we both work in the same clinic."

"You're kidding."

"No, but please don't take it personally. I once made the big mistake of getting involved with someone in the workplace. It was a disaster and I vowed never again."

"That's too bad. I think we could have a good time."

"I don't doubt it," she replied with a smile. "But I learned my lesson."

He nodded. "Fair enough. Have a nice day."

"You, too."

Breathing a sigh of relief, she headed for her next appointment. "Good morning, Ben," she said to the older gentleman as she entered the examining room. "How are you feeling?"

"Better now that you're here."

"I'm sorry you had to wait. One of our mares decided to have her foal this morning. I stayed until the vet arrived."

"You know how to deliver, too?"

Lily laughed. "All I could do was gentle her so she wouldn't panic."

"You're good at that, young lady, and beautiful, too. How come you're not married yet?"

There was an answer for that. But it was one she hadn't cared to think or talk about in years. "All the good ones like you are taken."

A chuckle escaped his lips. "One day some cowboy's going to stagger in here for help. He'll gaze into those periwinkle-colored eyes and fall head over heels. That's a promise."

She smiled indulgently. "Sounds good, Ben."

The sixty-two-year-old feed-store owner had been brought in two months ago almost crippled from mechanical back pain. After examining him, Lily had to train him how to lift and lower grain bags and other inventory that had caused his trouble over years of doing it wrong.

Lily patted the table. "Come on up and let's see how your exercises are progressing."

"You're going to be proud of me."

"I'm impressed how well you're moving." She put him through the procedures they'd been working on to strengthen his lower back. "Any pain?"

"Not anymore."

"All right, you can get down." He sat up the way she'd taught him and got off the table. "If all goes well and you remember what you have to do, I won't have to see you again."

"I don't like the sound of that. I'm going to miss you."

"You've been a terrific patient. I wish they were all like you. Good luck, Ben, and take care from now on."

"I intend to," he answered.

After he donned his Stetson and left the room, she disinfected the padded table and washed her hands to get ready for Janie Waters, her next appointment.

The thirty-five-year-old laundry worker suffered from mechanical back pain similar to Ben's. Because she'd always favored her left leg, which had once been broken, she'd created stress and needed to relearn movements to get rid of the pain while she was on her feet four hours a day. Once you broke or fractured a bone, you had to retrain the body how to move.

At eighteen, Lily had learned that lesson the hard way during the Vancouver Olympics, where she held a world downhill seventh ranking. Tragically, she'd crashed on the course and had to be airlifted to a local hospital. Not only did she have a compound fracture of the tibia, but she'd also jarred her back. The injury was called an acute facet spinal joint dysfunction.

After undergoing surgery, she'd been transferred to the University of Utah Hospital in Salt Lake City for expert treatment. Over the months that followed she started to recover, but not without a lot of therapy and a warning that another injury to her spine joint could cause paralysis.

The thought of never being able to walk again warred with her desire to start ski training again. As for getting pregnant one day, her doctor told her that pregnancy might bring on paralysis. That had been the other bad news. She'd discussed it with an obstetrician brought in for consultation, but it wasn't an issue in the foreseeable future.

At her lowest ebb, her parents had arranged for a psychiatrist while she was undergoing the rest of her therapy. The doctor wanted her to consider the possibility of finding a new career if she decided not to train again for the Olympics.

Though a cowgirl to the core, skiing had become a huge part of her life. She couldn't comprehend giving up her skis to attend college. After talking it over with her parents, she settled on getting her degree at the university in physiotherapy to help other injured athletes.

Interestingly enough she'd been introduced to hippotherapy on the back of a Missouri Fox Trotter kept on a ranch outside Salt Lake City. Known for its smooth gait for those suffering back pain, she and another patient had been elated with their results and had developed a passion for them during long comfortable rides.

After receiving her postgraduate degree, she returned home to Whitebark at twenty-six and went to work at the hospital. To her amazement, her parents purchased some Trotters they kept and bred on the ranch. She worked out an agreement with the hospital to assist some patients with hippotherapy at the ranch. A day didn't go by in this job that she didn't thank heaven for her parents. She could never repay them for all their love and devotion.

They'd arranged to give her an area at the back of the ranch house, where she could see patients young and old who needed this specialized therapy away from Whitebark Hospital. Lily derived a lot of satisfaction from helping injured teens performing in the junior rodeo who'd needed help with their pain before getting back to the sport they loved.

"Dr. Owens?" Her next patient's greeting from the doorway jarred her from her thoughts.

"Janie—how many times have I told you to call me Lily? I'm not a doctor. I'm a physiotherapist trained to help people overcome movement disorders."

"You're a damn good doctor to me!"

Lily chuckled. Janie Waters never minced words. "That's very nice to hear."

"It's the truth. I didn't think I'd ever be able to work at my job again until you helped me."

"So you're honestly doing better?"

"You'd know about it if I weren't." She got up on the table with ease and they went through some exercises together.

"I'm thrilled you're moving so much better."

"Yup. I'm up to three hours a day at work now."

When their session was over, her patient got off the table by herself.

"At this rate you'll be putting in your four hours in another month. Keep up the great work, Janie."

"I'm thankful for you, girl. See you in a week."

"You bet ya."

As Janie left, Lily went through the process of disinfecting the table and washing her hands again.

"Lily?" She swung around to discover Sharon Carter, a nurse from the orthopedic wing of the hospital, had just walked in. "I've brought you a new patient. Here's his file and X-rays. He came in on an emergency. Nothing's broken, but he'll need therapy. A word to the wise.

He's upset to have to be in here," she whispered. "Have fun, anyway." Her eyes danced.

"What do you mean?" she whispered back, but Sharon had already gone out to wheel her patient into the room.

"This is Ranger Ewing with the US Forest Service at Bridger-Teton," she announced. "Day before yesterday he was thrown from his horse in the middle of the night and had to wait hours for help. He was flown in by helicopter last evening and will tell you exactly what happened."

Sharon turned back to the patient and spoke in a soft, placating tone.

"Mr. Ewing? This is Lily, the physiotherapist who's going to help you get better. After you've had your consultation, one of the staff will wheel you back to your room." She pushed him over to Lily's desk.

"How soon can I be released?" The man's deep voice reached right through to Lily's insides.

"That depends on your therapist's diagnosis. I will now leave you in her care." Nodding briefly at them both, she walked out of the room and quietly shut the door behind her.

Lily found herself impaled by a pair of blazing dark brown eyes set in a face bronzed by the sun. He needed a shave and had a bruise on his right cheekbone. However, even in the robe-style blue hospital gown, or perhaps because of it, the blond-haired ranger had the kind of rugged good looks that could blow away every Hollywood heartthrob.

She couldn't help herself from dropping her gaze

to his muscular legs, which were bare below the hem of the gown, at his knees. She saw more bruises running along the side of his right leg. Judging by their length, and the size of his hands grasping the arms of the wheelchair, he had to be at least six foot two of pure rock-solid masculinity. The fact that his huge feet were adorned in hospital slippers only made his male charisma more potent.

She could sense his frustration and impatience. He was hurting, too. Besides the smile lines around his penetrating eyes, the creases around his compelling mouth were undoubtedly there because of pain.

Sucking in her breath, she asked, "Are you taking a painkiller at the moment?"

He lifted his head. In an instant, she felt him take her measure. "Yes."

"But it's not working."

"No."

"Is that because you're relying on ibuprofen instead of the drug your doctor prescribed?"

"Are you a mind reader, too?" he growled.

"No. I've been where you've been and hated to take any kind of medication. I'm afraid I'm the stubborn type, like you. I thought I could handle it."

"Touché." One corner of his mouth lifted, changing his demeanor. It was a sin for a man to be this handsome. Sharon's comment about having fun suddenly made sense.

Well, at least he wasn't so upset that he couldn't respond to a little humor.

Lily sat down in her chair. "Tell me what happened."

"I'd been up at the Crow's Nest trail doing a fire lookout watch with my partner."

"You lucky man. I used to go up there on my horse all the time, way above Fremont Lake. In summer there's no place like it—full of aspen groves, wildflowers and just plain jaw-dropping views."

"You're right." He sounded surprised she knew of it. "The tower sits just above Glimpse Lake. I was on my horse checking out an illegal campfire around two in the morning. After issuing the hunter some fines because, for one thing, he didn't have a permit to hunt deer, I confiscated his rifle and then ordered him to put out his illegal fire.

"Once he'd packed up his gear, I escorted him back to the tower, where we'd hold him until some more rangers came for him. But halfway there, my horse, Ace, stumbled over a hidden woodchuck burrow. It was so deep, I was thrown to the ground. My horse broke his leg and fell on top of me and the rifle, and was screaming in pain. The hunter took off and disappeared."

"You mean he just left you?" Lily gasped.

"He couldn't get away fast enough."

"I'm so sorry for your injuries." She shook her head. "And there's nothing worse than hearing a horse that's in unbearable agony."

"It was more excruciating than my own pain."

"I presume Ace was your close friend."

He eyed her intently. "Very close. He was amazing. I called headquarters for help because I was in too much pain to walk to the tower. They sent a helicopter with another ranger to take my place. The medics had to walk part way in.

"After a horrendous decision, we put the horse down and I was flown here. My truck and horse trailer are still up there. Among other things, I've got to be released so I can go after that hunter and arrest him."

She shuddered just thinking about it. "I don't blame you for being impatient. Give me a minute to look at your X-rays." She reached for the folder to study the film and read the radiologist's comments. Then she picked up his file.

Porter Ewing, US Forest Service.
    Date of birth: June 13. Twenty-seven, single, Caucasian, six-two, 220 pounds.
    78 West Juniper Road, Whitebark, Wyoming.

What it didn't say was that he had male charisma and charm no woman could be immune to.

She put down the file. "Tell me exactly how you fell."

"I went flying and landed on my right hip and arm. My cheek hit a rock. For a while I couldn't move, the pain was so bad. Finally with my left hand, I reached for my phone to make the emergency call."

"Have you tried walking on your own at all?"

"This morning I was wheeled to the shower and helped to stand for the thirty seconds it took."

"Okay. I'll wheel you to the bars over there." She reached in the drawer for a gait belt and walked around behind him. His big, broad shoulders distracted her as she pushed him across the room.

"The first thing I'm going to do is fasten this belt around your waist as a security caution." She showed him how it worked. "If you'll sit forward, I'll lock it."

He slowly did her bidding. When Lily reached around him, her awareness of him made it hard to concentrate. This wasn't supposed to happen when she was working with a patient. *Not ever.* Next, she put on the brake and adjusted the feet of the wheelchair.

"First, I want you to put your feet out flat, like this," she said, then demonstrated. "Good. Now, when I grip the belt on both sides of you, I want you to bend your knees and rely on your legs to stand. Don't try to use your back. Once you're upright, hold on to the bars while I do my exam. Ready?"

"Let's hope I don't fall on you." His eyes held a glint of amusement.

"I'm not worried." She slipped her hands inside his belt on either side of his body. "Now—one, two, three."

To her relief he got up with little problem while she gripped the belt, trapping her between him and the bars. At five foot six, she still had to look up a distance and could smell his minted breath.

"That was perfect." Lily let go of the gait belt and ducked under his strong arms. Standing at his side, she put her arm around his back. "I'm going to start touching you, and want to know the second you feel any pain."

Lily scrolled down his spine with her fingers like a cursor while she explored.

"I felt you wince, just now."

"I think that was a reaction to your touch."

Was he teasing her despite his pain?

She kept going until he made noise. "That gives me an idea of where your trauma is located." Another inch and he groaned. "*X* marks the spot, right?"

He nodded while the lines around his mouth deepened.

"That was all I needed to know." She ducked back under his arms and caught hold of the belt, breathing in the scent of the soap he'd used in the shower. "Remember to bend your legs and slowly sit down."

It was over in a flash. She undid the belt from around his waist and wheeled him back over to her desk. "Now that I know how I want to proceed, I'll ask the nurse to bring you back down here later this afternoon, after I've seen my last scheduled patient. Have them dress you in hospital pajamas.

"We'll do a few exercises to start working those muscles. I could tell you to take the stronger painkillers, but I know you won't. My greatest fear is that a stab of pain when you're not expecting it could freeze you up. But I'll let that be on your conscience, not mine."

He actually chuckled as she picked up the phone and asked the charge nurse on the orthopedic floor to send someone to take Ranger Ewing back to his room.

After she hung up, she caught him staring at her. "How soon will I be discharged from the hospital?"

"When you no longer require someone to help you get up and down, and you can stand and sit on your own without a gait belt," she answered firmly. "But you'll need a helper at home for at least a week. Perhaps your boss will give you a desk job you can do for a while."

"There's no way. I've got to go after that suspect."

"I don't blame you for being anxious, Mr. Ewing, but you have to follow through with your therapy. Starting next week, you'll have to come three times a week for two weeks, then we'll taper to two sessions a week. By six weeks, I'd like to think you'll be back to your old self."

He studied her so thoroughly, her pulse raced. "How long did it take you to recover from your injury?"

She wished she hadn't called attention to herself. "About four months."

"Why so long?"

"Part of my recovery was prolonged due to an infection after the surgery," she explained.

"What happened to you exactly?"

By now, Ron, one of the orderlies, who was a shameless flirt, had come in the room to take their patient back to his floor.

"I was skiing and crashed."

One eyebrow lifted in surprise. "You ski now?"

"Not anymore. See you this afternoon."

The orderly started to wheel the ranger out of the room. She heard Ron say, "Good luck trying to get information out of her." Then his voice grew fainter.

Stop talking, Ron. That was a painful period in her life she didn't want to remember if she could help it. It was a long time ago, and so many dreams had been shattered. Since coming home to Whitebark, she'd chosen not to look back.

In a minute, her next patient, Mr. Perry, an insurance man who'd fallen while out running, showed up. She

sighed. It was going to be a full day since she needed
to fit the strikingly handsome forest ranger into her
schedule.

Staying busy was the medicine she needed so she
wouldn't think about him. But that was a joke because
her visceral reaction to him had been a surprise. The
truth was, his nearness had stirred her senses—something that hadn't happened to her in years. She resented
it and would have to be on her guard from now on.

Ron pushed Porter inside his room. "How did it go
in physiotherapy?"

Porter didn't tell him what he thought about Lily,
who'd come as such a surprise that he still hadn't recovered. "I won't start exercises until later today."

"The clinic does a great job. While I'm here, do you
want me to help you in the bathroom?"

"Please."

After Porter was wheeled in and out, he was helped
into bed and left alone for a few minutes to contem-
plate his situation.

Since being transferred to Wyoming a year ago from
the Adirondacks in New York, where he'd been a forest
ranger and state trooper, Porter realized he had landed
in the best of all possible worlds. From the start he'd
learned to love the Wind River Mountain Range and
his assignments. It hadn't taken long to make the best
friends a man could have.

Funny how he'd thought he'd only last a year out
here. But three weeks after arriving in Whitebark, he'd
texted his mother in response to her query about rent-

ing the house. He'd told her he was selling the home in Lake Placid and planned to put roots down here in Wyoming. In his text he added, *The Wind Rivers is God's country west of the Continental Divide and I never want to live anywhere else. I'm putting my roots down here.*

His mother had been surprised because she'd deeded the house to him, thinking he'd want it one day. At that point they got on the phone to talk. She assured him he could keep renting the house or do whatever he wanted with it. Since the divorce and her marriage to her new husband, who was a widower and successful business-man, she didn't need the money from it.

The house, his legacy, had held painful memories for Porter because of his parents' divorce, and later on, his father's death. He couldn't go back to it. Hiring a Realtor to sell the house had been the right thing to do.

Porter knew it held painful memories for her too. It was a reminder of her marriage to his father, when she'd spent ninety percent of the time alone. Because he'd been a ranger and gone so often, she'd lived in a world of isolation. He loved his parents, but they should never have married. Living their lives apart had been no way to live. His mother, who preferred life in town, finally couldn't deal with it any longer.

From the proceeds of the sale, he'd bought the four-bedroom ranch house with a barn and paddock the guys had found for him here in Whitebark. It had a front lawn and flower beds. He liked the wraparound porch.

Most of all he loved the sight of Gannett Peak—the tallest peak in Wyoming—knifing up 13,804 feet in the thin atmosphere from his front yard. It always took his breath away. If Porter hadn't been an outdoors enthusiast like his father, he would probably have become a professional mountain climber, perhaps even running a climbing school. In his spare time, he'd probably ski.

The Wind River Mountain Range was Wyoming's largest, containing more than forty peaks over 13,000 feet. He planned to climb all of them one day and couldn't believe his luck in being transferred here from the Adirondacks. Though frustrated over the tragic accident that had killed his horse and incapacitated him for a little while, he had no right to complain about his life.

While deep in thought, his buddies walked in. Cole was an elk biologist, Wyatt, a sheep rancher, and Holden, the sheriff for Sublette County, Wyoming. One way or another the four of them had become close friends because of a serial arsonist that had plagued the ranchers of Sublette County last summer. Cole had been ingenious in identifying the culprits while the rest of them had been involved fighting the fires. From then on they'd worked, camped, hiked and skied together.

He was particularly fond of Wyatt's new wife, Alex. Like Porter, she'd come out to Wyoming from New York, but in her case she'd been sent out here on a magazine assignment. The two had fallen hard for each other, and their attitude about fly over country had been permanently changed.

Three of them, except Holden, were also volunteer firefighters for the Whitebark Fire Department, and all four men had been bachelors. But times had changed since then. Now, Porter was the only one not married and he was feeling it.

His spirits lifted when he saw them. "How did you guys know I was here?"

"News travels fast, buddy. You know that," Cole said with a smile. "We're sorry to hear about your accident. I talked to your boss. Stan has sent some rangers to bring your truck and trailer down to your house."

"I'll have to thank him for that."

"We're sorry about your horse," Wyatt interjected.

Porter's eyes closed tightly for a moment. "If you could have heard Ace…he was in so much agony he had to be put down."

All three men commiserated. "Thank heaven you're all right and didn't break any bones."

"It was a miracle, Holden, but that vagrant needs to be caught. I've got to get out of here and go after him."

Cole sat forward. "I hear you, but the nurse said you're going to need physiotherapy."

"I know. It'll take up some of my time, but I realize it's necessary. I hurt when I move the wrong way. My first workout will be later in the day." The guys had no idea how eager Porter was to see Lily again.

"That's good. We want you back on your feet for the campout we've got planned for the Fourth of July next month. Tonight we'll come over and have dinner with you. Can we bring you anything?"

Porter's mind was still on the pretty therapist. "Would it be possible if one of you could drop by the ranch house first? I need my laptop and toiletries."

Wyatt nodded. "Consider it done. Anything else?"

"That's more than enough."

An orderly from the kitchen came in the room with his lunch tray. "Why don't you eat with me?"

Holden stood up first. "I've got to get going to the jail, but we'll be here at dinnertime."

"Thanks, guys. I owe you."

After they left, he turned on the TV and ate the chicken-fried steak. He didn't have to be on a particular diet. The last time he remembered being in a hospital, he was eight years old getting his tonsils out.

Though it would take a long time for him to get over the loss of his horse, he could cope. Plus his day had brightened when he realized he'd be spending time with the hospital's physiotherapist. She had to be Whitebark's best-kept secret.

When he thought back over the last year, he couldn't recall any of his friends or coworkers needing a physiotherapist. There'd been no talk of a gorgeous one working at this hospital. If Porter had a problem, it was going to be his lack of patience before going to his next therapy session.

Maybe the accident had done something to his psyche because he'd never been this attracted to a woman in his life. Porter had dated his share of women back east and here in Whitebark, but what he did for a living was unique.

It would take a special kind of woman who wanted to settle down with him and raise a family in rugged country like this. He hadn't met a woman who fit the picture he'd always had in his mind.

Until now…

After eating, he made a phone call to Stan Fitzer at headquarters. His boss was the head of the forest service for the Bridger-Teton forest of the Wind Rivers. After giving Stan an update, he watched several documentaries on the Yellowstone volcanic caldera and another on the volcanic eruption on Mt. St. Helens in Washington State. They kept him semi-entertained, but he was counting the minutes until it was time for his first workout.

Like clockwork, Ron came in at four. He helped him into hospital pajamas and supported him into the wheelchair. Then he wheeled him down to the clinic. Since meeting the stunning therapist, Porter wanted to know more about her.

"Do you know why Lily has stopped skiing?" he asked the orderly. His mind was still filled with the vision of her neck-length shimmering black hair—the fragrance had reminded him of the wildflowers she'd gushed about.

"I once tried to find out after one of the nurses told me she wasn't married, but she keeps to herself."

"How long have you known her?"

"I started working here six months ago, and she joined the hospital about three months ago," Ron answered. "But I could never even get to first base with her."

What man wouldn't try who still had his sight?

Chapter 2

"Knock, knock."

"Come on in, Ron."

As Porter was wheeled in, he saw Lily at her desk typing information into the computer.

She got up from the chair and turned around. Her gaze flew to Porter's. She had to be the only woman he'd ever met with eyes the color of the damask violets that grew in the higher altitudes of the mountains.

"Mr. Ewing—" She walked toward him with the belt. "Don't you look smashing in your jammies."

He hadn't heard that word in years. "I like them, too. My name is Porter by the way." Good grief, she was beautiful. "Mind if I call you Lily?"

"I prefer it. How are you feeling?"

"Anxious to get started." It surprised him that he

wasn't in more pain. With that belt, the 120-pound beauty had helped him stand and sit as if he weighed nothing.

"Let's hope you feel this way every time you come."

"Is there a chance that I won't?"

"I'll never tell," she teased and wheeled him over to a pad on the floor. After setting the brake and turning out the feet, she stood in front of him with the belt. "You know the drill. Sit forward." She was all business.

He could feel his pulse pick up speed just anticipating it. With a smile, he raised his arms so she could fasten it around his waist. His body was sore everywhere, but he hardly noticed with her arms around him, bringing them breathtakingly close.

"Now place your feet on the floor the way I showed you." Porter followed her instructions. "Ready? Knees bent?"

He looked into her eyes. "Whenever you are."

Averting her gaze, she reached to hold on to the belt. A tiny nerve throbbed at the base of her throat above her yellow top. He was curious to know if it was a normal reaction. *Or not.* "One, two, three."

Porter rose to his feet with a minimum of pain. She still had hold of him. "Step on the pad and get down on your knees while I support you with the belt." He carefully responded. "Now slowly put your hands down on the pad. As you start to slide, extend your left arm so you can turn over. I'll help you."

He was amazed that he could move with only small twinges of discomfort. Once on his back, she kneeled at his feet and started his exercises. She lifted one leg, then the other.

"Let me know the second it hurts." To his surprise he experienced almost no pain.

"In a few weeks we'll start some hippotherapy since I know riding a horse is part of your job. But right now I don't want that region to get irritated." She walked around and kneeled at his side, allowing him the chance to study her lovely mouth and high cheekbones. "How are you feeling? Have you had enough?"

If she had any idea what her nearness was doing to him and how much he enjoyed her hands on his legs, she'd run from him and never come back.

"Is there a time limit?"

"Yes, but I don't want you to overdo it your first time. However, *you're* the patient and have to let me know how you are feeling."

"I think I can handle two more times with each leg." She smiled. "Let's do it."

His heart rate kicked up before she got into her other position to finish up. In the next breath she was at his side again. "All right, now put out your arm and we'll get you turned over."

Again he was surprised that exercise hadn't made him sore. When he'd accomplished what she asked, Lily said, "Now back up with your hands and slowly rise up on your knees." She kept her hands tucked into his belt. "Ready?" she asked when he was in position. "I'm going to help you stand."

Using the technique of bending his legs and not relying on his back, he got to his feet, virtually free of residual pain. She held on to the belt until he'd situated himself in the wheelchair.

"Good job! Mission accomplished, Porter." Her full smile lit up his universe.

"Your magic has made a believer out of me."

She cocked her head, causing that luscious black hair to swing back and forth. "It's the pure science of movement. You thought this was all going to be foolishness?"

"No. But when Ace landed on top of me, I feared I might end up in a wheelchair for life."

She wheeled him over to the desk. "As you can see, you've already moved on your own without crying out in pain. In another day or two your strength will have returned and you won't need the belt. If you'll undo it, I'll put it away."

Porter didn't want this session to be over, but she was waiting. He unfastened it while she reached for the ends and lifted it from his body. Next she phoned for someone to come for him.

"Ron will be here any minute for you."

"Do you have more patients coming?"

"No. You were my last one. I'll see you again in the morning at ten." That good news would help him get through the night.

To his frustration she sat down in her swivel chair and started putting information into the computer. Maybe he was wrong, but he had a feeling it was on purpose and secretly hoped his nearness disturbed her, too. He wasn't about to let her ignore him no matter how hard she tried.

"Yours is a very physical job. I would imagine there

are evenings when you go home exhausted." Was she involved with someone?

"There are times."

Another half minute passed before he said, "Are you going to leave me in suspense?"

She turned in her swivel chair, looking startled. "What do you mean?"

"This morning you told me you survived a crash. I've been curious ever since. Did it happen at the White Pines ski area?" It was where he and his buddies liked to ski during the winter when they could get away.

"No. Whistler, Canada."

That surprised him. "Were you there on vacation?"

"No. I was racing in the Olympics."

He took a quick breath. "You were on the Olympic team? How old were you?"

"Eighteen. But I crashed during the Super G and it put me out of commission."

Porter shook his head, utterly blown away. "How long ago was that?"

"Eight years back."

So that meant she was twenty-six. "How did it happen?"

"Surely you don't want to know."

"Actually I do. I happen to be crazy about skiing myself. Normally I watch the Olympics, but eight years ago my parents were going through a painful divorce. As a result, I missed it."

Compassion filled her beautiful violet eyes. "I'm sorry for that, Porter. I can't imagine anything more painful than watching your parents break up." She sounded like she meant it.

"It was awful, but I'm the one who's sorry for your accident that ended years of training to become a part of the team. What went wrong?"

She let out a little sigh. "About thirty seconds into my run, I made a left-footed turn and arced my skis to the right, but I had to manage a jump at the same time. At that point I was off balance and had an unstable landing. The minute I hit the snow, my left leg skidded to the left and my knee hyperextended.

"I pitched forward and began to tumble. My boot came off before I slammed into the barrier. I was airlifted to the hospital and learned I'd broken my leg. My tibia bone pierced through the skin and my leg still has screws. But the worst part was the jarring of my spine joint. The surgeon warned me that if I injured it again, I'd be paralyzed. So I gave up skiing."

Porter was horrified by what she'd told him. She'd been forced to give up skiing. But at what cost to her, mentally and emotionally?

"No one would ever know your story of survival or your heartache by looking at you."

"Heartache is right. Once I was stable, I was flown to the university hospital in Salt Lake City. The doctors there took marvelous care of me and I recovered. Because of their expertise, I decided to become a physiotherapist, like the people who'd worked on me." Lifting her chin ever so slightly, she said, "I hope that has answered all your questions."

He hadn't even begun to scratch the surface, but he

would have to wait until tomorrow because Ron had just come in the room. Porter eyed her solemnly. "Thank you for today's workout, Lily, and for sharing with me. I'll see you in the morning."

He turned to Ron in a completely different frame of mind than when he'd been wheeled down for this session. Lily had overcome a tragedy that could have ruined the life of someone who wasn't a warrior.

Later that evening after his friends had eaten with him and left, he opened his laptop, logged onto Wi-Fi and searched for video clips of the Vancouver Olympics on YouTube. There were dozens of them. He narrowed his search to the alpine events until he came to the Super G.

Spectacular Crash Sends Lily Owens to the Hospital

Bingo. He clicked on the video and heard a short history about the young and attractive, new alpine sensation from Wyoming. Porter was riveted and horrified all over again as he watched what happened exactly the way she'd told him. He cringed to watch another video showing her being helped off the piste to an ambulance.

The announcer mentioned she'd lost consciousness for a few minutes, a detail she hadn't told Porter. That meant she'd suffered a concussion, among other things. Lily had been rated seventh in the running for the Super G event before her spectacular crash only thirty seconds out of the start gate. What a terrible loss to the ski-racing world.

He watched some of the racers in her event before

closing his laptop. To have survived that crash and live to tell about it was a miracle in and of itself. But to see her in person today, moving and functioning so normally to help others with injuries, he thought she epitomized human triumph in his eyes.

After the nurse came in to check his vital signs and get him ready for bed, he took some ibuprofen and put his head on the pillow, but he knew sleep wouldn't come for a long time.

Lily's day at the hospital started at eight thirty every weekday morning except for Wednesdays, when she did the afternoon shift and stayed through to seven o'clock for emergencies.

This Tuesday morning shouldn't have been any different from all the others, but for a reason she didn't want to admit, she'd had trouble deciding what to wear while she got ready. It was the ranger's damn fault. After all her years of training, she didn't dare get involved with a patient. Lily shouldn't care what he thought about her.

After her shower she decided on a pale blue short-sleeved top and matching denims. Silly really for her to even think about it since she wore a lab coat over her clothes and technician's nonslip shoes. But when she looked in the mirror to put on her tiny flowered blue earrings, she frowned.

The side part of her layered bob gave her a slight bang, a boring style she hadn't bothered to change in a couple of years. Maybe it was time for a new style, something a little shorter, possibly a windswept look that would be easier to take care of. Later today she'd call Millie at Style Clips and make an appointment.

Millie Edwards, her closest friend from grade school, was now married and expecting a baby. Before Millie had to cut down her hours in preparation for the blessed event, Lily needed to get over there. Her friend would know exactly what style would suit her. Maybe they could go to lunch today.

After applying lipstick, she left her second-floor bedroom at the rear of the ranch house and hurried out to the garage to her silver Volkswagen Passat convertible. Lily had bought it as a present to herself from the money she'd been earning. She sped off and left the top down, loving the breeze against her face and hair, a holdover from the days when she stepped out of the blocks to fly down the mountain.

There was no way she could ever reimburse her parents for everything they'd done for her. But since working at the hospital, she'd insisted on buying the things she needed and paid her parents rent for living there. Those were some of the things she *could* do to justify her existence.

Halfway to the drive-thru where she often bought breakfast, it dawned on her that she hadn't checked on the new foal, or gone to the barn to walk Trixie out to the corral. That was a first, which wasn't very nice to her horse.

Of course, Stuart, the man who managed the ranch, would take care of her mare, along with all the other horses. But it surprised her that her mind had been somewhere else this morning. Thinking about her newest patient went against all the rules. She could get fired from her position by the higher-ups and needed to fight her attraction with all her might.

Lily grabbed coffee and a breakfast burrito and headed to the hospital, where she put on a fresh lab coat. Her first appointment was Judge Jenkins, who'd been in a recent car accident. He'd been T-boned by a truck. Luckily no bones had been broken, but he was in a lot of distress.

"Hi, Judge! How's it going?"

"You don't want to know."

Lily laughed. "Oh, but I do. How else will I be able to help you? Let's get you down on the pad so we can work out the kinks."

"What I need is a new body."

She helped him get settled. How many hundreds of times had she wished for the same thing after her crash? "There's nothing wrong with this one that a little more therapy won't make better."

"Who made you such an optimist?" he asked good-naturedly.

"It goes with the business." But only after years of deciding she had to become one if she was going to make it through the rest of her life.

While she worked with him, her mind was counting down to ten o'clock, something she'd rarely done before the arrival of the ranger. This *had* to stop.

When her patient finally left, she heard him talking in the hall with another man who called him "Judge." The next thing she knew, Sharon wheeled in the ranger. The mere sight of him made her pulse race.

"Hey, Lily. Got another one for you. See you later."

"Thanks, Sharon."

This morning her handsome patient was already dressed in hospital pajamas. As her eyes wandered over him, she realized that he'd shaved. Above his chiseled jaw she also noticed that the lines of pain had faded somewhat from around his mouth.

"Good morning, Lily." His deep voice penetrated her senses the same way it had yesterday, but she detected a difference in his demeanor. "I didn't realize Judge Jenkins was a patient of yours."

"Do you know him?"

"Only in the sense that one of my best friends is working with him to put a killer in prison. The judge is a good man."

"I agree." She stood up. "From the looks of it, I'd say you slept well last night. Are you ready for another workout?" She pulled the gait belt out of the drawer.

"I've been looking forward to it."

So had she, though she'd tried hard not to. "All right, let's get started." She pushed him over to the floor pad and set the brake.

"Why don't I put that around my waist myself?"

"If you feel you can." She handed it to him. "But stop the second it hurts too much. Of course, knowing you, I'm afraid you won't admit to pain, but there'll be other ways I can tell."

His dark eyes searched hers. "How?"

"That's my secret."

A slow smile broke out on his face before he leaned forward and used his left arm to push one end around the back of his body. Then he used his right arm, the one with the bruises, to grab it, and fastened both ends.

"Bravo, Porter. I know that hurt when I saw the lines around your mouth deepen for a moment, but I'm convinced it didn't do any damage."

Their eyes met and held. "Yesterday I couldn't have done that, which means I'm getting better under your care."

"You keep up that attitude, Porter, and you'll be back at the fire lookout in no time."

"If I didn't know better, I'd think you were anxious to get rid of me."

"I am," Lily responded. "I know you're itching to return to work so you can catch that culprit who left you to die in the dark." She paused. "Now remember what we went through yesterday. Lean forward a little. Make sure your feet are firmly planted on the floor and bend your legs." As she took hold of the belt, she detected the scent of lime, probably from his shaving gel. "Okay. Here we go."

He was up a little faster than yesterday, and moved into position before getting down on his knees. Without her giving him instructions, he did everything right and turned over on his back.

She looked down at him before getting on her knees to take hold of his left leg. "I think you're a fraud."

He chuckled, a low, rumbling sound that excited her. To her dismay she found everything about him enticing. This attraction to him was *all* wrong. After her involvement with Steve Louter during the Olympics, she'd sworn off men.

They did a workout that was ten minutes longer than yesterday. She pushed him, but his body didn't tense.

"What's the prognosis, Lily?"

"Your body is healing, otherwise we couldn't have gone this long. But you've done enough for this morning."

"Will I be seeing you later today?"

Yes. She got to her feet. "You've been scheduled for three o'clock. Are you ready to get back in the wheelchair?"

"Whenever you are."

"Your stamina is remarkable." So remarkable he might not take as long to go back to his full-time duties.

He turned over carefully and got into position for her to help lift him. She leaned down to grasp the belt. By accident her cheek brushed against his, sending an electric current through her body. This time when he stood to his full height, she knew that by tomorrow he wouldn't need the belt.

Once he was settled in the chair, he removed it without her asking. She took off the brake and rolled him to her desk. After calling for an orderly to come and get him, she put the belt back in the drawer.

"Do you have another patient before lunch?"

"Yes. A teen who collided with another player at his high school's last game of the season in February. He fell hard on his left hip and needs occasional therapy so he can go out for training in August."

"Did they win?"

His sense of humor made her laugh. "As a matter of fact, they did."

"Then he'll get better faster."

"So speaks Dr. Ewing. I didn't know you were a psychiatrist, too."

"More a student of human nature. Some injuries have to be harder to overcome than others." Clearing his throat, he said softly, "Last night I watched some videos of you on my laptop. I hope you won't be offended if I told you my heart came close to failing me when I saw you come down that course and crash. I admire you more than you know for what you've endured and become."

Shocked that he'd looked at the videos—let alone that he'd said those things to her—she turned to him. "There are millions of athletes in every field who go through the same thing year in and year out. Some of them have suffered injuries so much worse than mine. Don't make me out to be a saint, Porter."

"I'm not, but I believe in giving credit where it's due. What I've been asking myself is that if something that death-defying had happened to me at the age of eighteen, could I have pulled myself out of it the way you did? But naturally, it's uncomfortable for you to talk about. I promise I won't bring it up again." He looked at her through shuttered eyes. "Forgive me?"

She took a deep breath. "There's nothing to forgive. It's my fault for talking about myself when we were discussing painkillers. You wouldn't be human if you weren't curious. The internet exists for humankind's successes and failures to be revealed."

"Do you wish there weren't such a thing?"

Lily smiled. "Not at all. It beats doing things the old-fashioned way, like going to the library and looking up information in the card catalog."

"You're not old enough to remember that far back."

"You're right, but I heard my nana talk about the times she did research for a local radio show. She hosted it from Jackson Hole about the Old West after my grandfather died. He'd been a big hunter and had a lot of information for her from his family memorabilia.

"The one thing I remember was that she complained about only being able to take ten books home from the library to read at a time. Worse, half the ones she'd been waiting for to come in hadn't been returned on time. But somehow she did it for five years."

"She must have been popular to stay on the air that long. Is she still alive?"

"I'm afraid she passed away when I was sixteen. My nana grew up on her parents' Jackson Hole ranch and became a champion barrel racer in the rodeo. She reigned supreme for a long time. We did a lot of riding together. I loved her to death."

"What about your mom?"

"She preferred skiing and became an Olympian. She met my father, who was also an Olympian. When I was two, they started teaching me."

Porter was quiet for a moment, then said, "Dare I say I'm more impressed than ever. Greatness runs in your family."

"My parents are the great ones. *Their* story is remarkable for the kindness and devotion they've shown to me. In my opinion they're the true saints of this world."

"Knock, knock."

Ron! Lily had completely forgotten about him. It was a good thing he'd come. She'd been talking her head off because Porter had a way of pulling information out of her.

"Come on in," she called to the orderly. "My patient is ready to go. See you at three."

Once they went out the door, Lily put more information in the computer. She still trembled as she remembered the feel of Porter's jaw coming in contact with the side of her face.

After she got up to wash her hands, she reached for her cell and phoned her friend Millie. She couldn't go to lunch today, but Lily made a hair appointment for the following morning at nine and they would have a good talk then. Once they'd hung up, her office phone rang.

"Yes, Cindy?"

"Two things. Your eleven-thirty appointment just canceled due to stomach flu and will reschedule. Also, a Mr. Fitzer, the head of the forest service, is here and wants to know if he can have a brief word with you about Ranger Ewing."

Her heartbeat sped up. "Of course. I'm free now. Send him in."

Chapter 3

Porter remained in the wheelchair to eat his lunch and was deep in thought over Lily when he heard his name called. He looked up, expecting to see the nurse or Ron. Instead it was his boss.

"Stan—"

"How are you doing?"

"Better than expected."

"Knowing about your accident, I didn't think I'd see you in this good of shape," Stan admitted. "But after meeting your therapist and learning of today's progress, I know why."

"You've talked to Lily?" The question shot out of his mouth before he could stop it.

His boss smiled. "*If* she's the one with violet eyes and black hair." Porter had walked into that one. "According to her, you'll probably be released to go home day after tomorrow."

That was good news, *and bad.* He liked it that she was only a floor away from him.

"She recommends a health-care aide to be with you for the first week, one who can drive you to your therapy sessions. I'll arrange for that service. And when the week is out, we'll talk about your coming back to work at a desk job."

"I don't think I'll have to be home a whole week." As Lily had reminded him, the culprit had left him to die. Porter needed to go after him ASAP.

"That's her decision. Your therapist comes highly recommended here in the state of Wyoming."

Porter believed it, but he would still do his best to change her mind. He'd go crazy without work. "I appreciate your coming by. I'll be back before you know it."

"Don't rush it, Porter. Follow the rules." At the doorway, he paused. "I want you to return to the department when you're ready, not before. At that point we'll talk about getting you another horse." Porter had wondered how long it would take before he could even ride one again.

As for Ace, he would be impossible to replace. They'd functioned as one. It would take time to break in a new horse and start over again.

"Thank you for everything, Stan."

"So long." He disappeared out the door.

Feeling stronger, Porter wheeled himself over to the bed and turned on the TV. He watched the news until Ron came to help him shower. It was no longer a painful ordeal, just a few twinges. After that he decided to phone his mother who'd moved to Buffalo, New York, with her new husband. She would want to know what had happened to him.

The phone call went pretty much as expected. His mother rejoiced that nothing was broken. They both lamented over the loss of his horse. Her next reaction was to tell him she would fly out and take care of him—she claimed he wouldn't need a health giver when he had her.

Porter thanked her for the offer but assured her he didn't plan to be home that long. "I have friends who've already been helping me. When I'm recovered, I have a week's vacation coming up in August and will fly out to see you and Art."

"You promise?"

"Have I ever broken one?"

"I can't help but worry about you," his mother grumbled. "Do you believe that this therapist is giving you the proper help?"

"She's reputed to be the best in the state, otherwise my boss wouldn't have had the helicopter fly me to this hospital and clinic."

"Well, I guess I have to trust you to know what you're doing. But I'm going to pester you every day until I know you're fully recovered and back to doing what you love."

He smiled. "I'll look forward to every phone call. I want to hear what you and Art have been up to. Give him my best. Love you, Mom."

Porter had barely hung up when it was time to see

Lily again. Ron was the one to wheel him down to the clinic. They had to wait outside until the therapy room door opened. When it did, Porter saw and heard a man in his thirties who was talking to her.

"The next time I come, I'll convince you to go to dinner with me."

"It's against the rules, Mr. Lattimer, but thank you for asking."

He shook his head. "I'm not giving up."

On his way out, he almost bumped into Ron. The man's interest didn't surprise Porter. Lily had apparently been attracting the attention of male admirers for years. He'd seen more evidence of it today as he witnessed his boss's reaction to her.

Ron had said she was still single, but that told him next to nothing about her love life. Porter was determined to find out more.

When Ron wheeled him in the room, Lily was standing there waiting for him with the belt in hand. Anyone not knowing the situation would think she was waiting to flay her next victim.

He decided she'd read his mind, because she said, "You're back for more torture?"

"I can handle it."

She set his brake. "That's what I told your boss when he talked to me earlier. He's says you're pretty indispensable around the department. I understand your former boss in the Adirondacks hated letting you go and wants you back."

That must have been quite a conversation. "What other skeletons did he let out of the closet?"

"I guess you have a few of them then?" she teased. "I knew you hadn't grown up out here. I should have recognized your New York accent."

"Is it that strong?"

A quick smile appeared. "Once in a while something slips out that lets me know you're not from the Wild West." She handed him the belt. He put it on with even less difficulty than this morning. "What part of New York do you come from?"

He fastened it. "Lake Placid." Emotion darkened her eyes to a deep purple.

A connection had been made. "Did you know the old Olympic village is now a federal prison?"

"I heard as much, but I've never skied there. Did you grow up on skis, too?"

"Skis and horses," he replied. "They were a necessity for my father, a ranger who worked for the fish-and-game industry all his adult life. I simply followed in his footsteps."

"The Adirondacks is such a beautiful area of the country. I'm surprised you left to come out here."

Porter's eyes narrowed on her. "That's one of the skeletons in my closet."

"We all have skeletons," she murmured.

He continued to stare at her. "You mean you haven't revealed the rest of yours to me?"

When she went quiet, Porter realized he'd hit a nerve, and she'd closed herself up. After the long pause, she said, "Why don't we get started."

He put his feet on the floor the way she'd taught him and waited for her to grab hold of the belt to help him.

When he was standing, she held on while they walked in measured steps over to the pad.

For the next twenty minutes she worked with him. He found it easier to move and was disappointed when she helped him back in the wheelchair.

"How do you feel?"

He handed her the belt. "Surprisingly good. Today I haven't even taken ibuprofen."

"But you might notice a few aches in bed tonight. I worked you harder this last session. You might need some yet."

"I don't think so."

She studied his right arm. "Your bruises are starting to turn a yellowish gray color. That's a good sign."

"On my cheek, too."

Her gaze lifted to his face. "It's starting to fade. Pretty soon you'll be able to lie on your right side."

"How do you know which side I prefer when I sleep?"

"I don't, but most of us have a favorite position in bed."

To his amusement color swept into her cheeks. She turned to phone for an orderly to come and get him. After she hung up, he asked, "What's yours?"

Laughter broke from her. "You must have driven your mother crazy when you were a little boy."

"I still do, but you haven't answered my question."

She sat down on her chair. "I guess I like lying on my stomach. After skiing, I used to lie facedown on a pillow and fall asleep exhausted in front of the TV."

"Sounds good. I'm looking forward to doing that myself."

"It won't be long."

A moment later, Ron walked in the room. "Ready to go back upstairs?"

"You arrived just in time. He's dying for relief from his taskmaster," she answered while putting information in the computer. "See you tomorrow, Porter."

"Have a good evening, Lily."

She knew damn well the last thing he wanted was for this conversation to end. As he was wheeled out into the hall, his gut sensed that she didn't want him to leave, either. What saved the day for him was knowing he had two more sessions tomorrow, plus five weeks of therapy with her. By then, anything could happen.

After going on a horseback ride with her mom Wednesday morning, Lily showered, ate a quick breakfast with her dad and left in her car for Style Clips. She'd found a couple of hairstyles online that she'd printed off to show Millie.

When she walked inside, she hugged her friend, who'd started to show. "I'm so excited for you. While I'm here, let's pick a day for the baby shower. You come up with the guest list and I'll get the invitations sent out. We'll do it at the ranch."

"You don't have to give me a shower."

"I can't believe you just said that! You're my very best friend. Pretty soon you're going to have a sweet little girl and I want to celebrate that."

Millie teared up and hugged her again. "Okay. Enough about me. Do you want the same old?"

"No." Lily opened her purse and showed her the papers with the two different hairstyles.

Her friend's eyes widened. "Both of these would look terrific on you. What's happened for you to want such a drastic change after all this time?"

"Because I've worn the same hairstyle since I was eighteen, and it makes me feel old."

Millie's eyebrows lifted. "Sounds like you've met a guy."

Lily hated it when her cheeks grew warm and gave her away. "What do you mean?" She sat down in the chair Millie always used.

"Exactly what I said. Who is he?" She put the drape around her neck.

For the time being, they were the only two in the salon. "A patient."

"How long has he been coming to you?" her friend asked.

"I've had four sessions with him since Monday."

"And it's only Wednesday. Is he a looker?"

Lily looked in the mirror at her friend. "I'm afraid so. The jaw-dropping kind I've sworn off. Tall and muscular with blond hair and dark brown eyes." She sighed. "The total package."

"What does he do for a living?"

"He's a forest ranger who got transferred here from Lake Placid, New York."

"Ah. An easterner. How long ago?"

"I don't know."

"I think I've heard about a ranger who's a real hottie. Why did he come?"

"That's something else I don't know yet, but I'm convinced there's a story somewhere."

Millie tipped her back so she could wash her hair. "After Steve's colossal sin of omission, don't you think you'd better find out before you lose your heart again?"

"Right now he's just a patient. You know the hospital rules. I would never date a man from my workplace or a patient. This ranger is a charmer, but so far he hasn't done anything to make me believe he's interested, except to get better as fast as possible." She worried her bottom lip. "I'm afraid he's pushing himself too hard. But he has made me take another look at myself and change my boring appearance."

Her friend laughed as if her comment was ridiculous. "How much does he know about you?"

"It slipped out that I used to ski."

"Used to—" Millie's eyes widened. *"Does he know what happened in Whistler?"*

"He told me he watched some video clips."

"And you tell me he's not interested," her friend said, and tsked.

"I meant that he's…different."

"You mean he hasn't hit on you yet."

"No," Lily said.

"Have you told him about Steve?"

"No."

"You'd better watch this one. He's playing it cool and knows what he's doing. Just promise me you won't let him hurt you." Once she was sitting up again, Millie dried Lily's hair enough to comb through it. "Already he's got you wanting me to change your hairstyle. Which one do you like best?"

Lily could see them propped against the mirror. "Both."

"I think I'll do a cross between the two of them. But you'd better be sure before I start cutting."

"I *am* sure. I feel like everyone else is getting on with life but me." She gestured toward her friend. "Look at you. Married and having a baby. Nothing's happening to me."

"You're so funny. It already has!"

"Except that he's off-limits." Her conversation with Porter about skeletons in their closets had disturbed her. "Oh, let's drop the subject. How about we do a shower at the ranch a week from Thursday?"

"That would be perfect, but stop putting me off. Won't you at least tell me the name of your mystery patient?"

"It's Ranger Ewing."

"*Porter* Ewing?"

"Yes."

The scissors almost fell from Millie's hand. "You're kidding!"

"What's wrong?"

"Jessica married Sheriff Granger and it turns out he and Porter Ewing are best friends."

Both Jessica and Millie worked in this shop, owned by Jessica's mother. "Even if that's true, it has nothing to do with me."

"I could ask her some questions and find out if she knows anything about the ranger you're treating."

"I'd rather you didn't, Millie. Please. This has to stay between us."

Her friend huffed out a breath. "All right. I won't say a word."

"Thank you."

She closed her eyes as Millie started to cut. Holden Granger had been the sheriff of Whitebark for quite a while. Lily didn't know him personally, but she'd heard of his sterling reputation through her father.

If Porter was a friend of his, that had to account for something. But it still didn't mean anything if there was a dark secret in his past he didn't want to be known, not even to a best friend.

It wasn't fair to assume something was wrong, but after Steve, Millie was right. You couldn't be too careful and Lily was a fool to go on entertaining thoughts about him.

A few minutes before ten a.m., Ron helped Porter into the wheelchair and pushed him down to the clinic. This morning he'd been able to stay in the shower for a few minutes and didn't require Ron's help getting in or standing.

His close friends and a couple of the other forest rangers had come over to visit the night before and they'd talked shop until the nurse told them visiting hours were over. It all helped to pass the time until he saw Lily again.

While in the hallway, Ron stopped in front of another door that was open. "Dr. Jensen?" he called out. "I've brought Mr. Ewing."

"Fine. Bring him in."

Porter frowned. "Where's Ms. Owens?" he asked the other man after Ron left.

"She only works afternoons on Wednesday." Porter's spirits plummeted. "I'm the head of the clinic and have read up on her charting. Don't worry. I'll carry out her plans for you to the letter."

"I'm sure you will. I was only surprised." She hadn't said a word about not being here this morning.

"I understand." He felt the doctor's eyes appraise him. Porter got the distinct impression he didn't like him. "When a patient gets used to his therapist, it's hard to accept change, even for one visit." With that comment, Porter understood. The doctor had a thing for her. Well, join the club. "As far as I know, she plans to keep her three-o'clock appointment with you."

They went through the same routine he did with Lily, but it wasn't the same. It *couldn't* be, not in a million years.

"You're coming along, Mr. Ewing, just as she said."

"Thank you, Dr. Jensen."

"My pleasure."

Like hell it was. By the time Ron came for him, Porter was jumping out of his skin. They went up to his room, where he ate lunch. At this point he was in a foul mood and it was agony waiting for three o'clock to roll around. What if she didn't come? If he had to do his therapy with Dr. Jensen again, he'd make up the excuse that he wasn't feeling well to avoid it.

When Ron showed up in his room at five to three,

Porter asked, "Do you know if Lily is going to be here for my appointment?"

"Let me check."

He came back a minute later. "She's there. How come you asked?"

"She wasn't here this morning. I'd rather work with her than anyone else."

The other man grinned. "I can't blame you for that. Let's go."

His adrenaline surged as Ron wheeled him downstairs to the examining room and knocked.

"Come on in."

Both men saw her at the same time seated at her desk, but it was Ron who said, "Wow! I hardly recognize you with that new hairdo."

She smiled. "Is that good or bad?"

"Oh, it's good, all right!"

"Thank you."

After Ron left, she stood up. "How did it go with Dr. Jensen this morning?"

Today she'd worn a white blouse beneath her lab coat. She always looked fresh and smelled marvelous. Porter was still studying her hair, which had been styled in a feathery cut. It looked so sensational on her, he was tongue-tied.

"I'm afraid I upset him when I asked where you were. It went well, but he doesn't have your touch." Porter would never forget the first time she'd touched him and the sensations that had passed through him.

She avoided his eyes. "I just read the notes he sent to my computer. He agrees with me that we should forego the belt this afternoon and see how you get along. If you feel strong enough, why don't you wheel yourself to the pad."

On his own steam he crossed the room, forcing him to use more muscles, but he felt no discomfort. She leaned over to set the brake. He had to suppress the urge to plunge his hands into her glossy black hair and pull her onto his lap. If he ever started kissing her, he'd never stop.

"Before you get up, think of all the steps. Remember I'm right here to steady you should you feel the slightest weakness or pain. I'll stand by you, Porter, ready to help."

He concentrated on what he had to do and stood up without using his back. Her tricks were working. He bent his legs again and got down on his knees, following her instructions. Incredible how well he moved. The all-over soreness was easing.

She kneeled down and put him through his exercises. Her new hairstyle revealed the contours of her oval face and accentuated those dark-fringed lilac eyes he'd fallen in love with. Again he marveled at her gentle touch. She was careful not to hurt the bruising on his right leg, and knew just the right amount of pressure to exert.

When he thought about it, if he'd never received therapy, he would never have met her and could have done so much damage by moving the wrong way.

"All right, we're through for today."

He didn't want it to be over. What he wished he'd dare do was pull her down with him. But that would end everything, and he couldn't allow that to happen if he hoped to continue seeing her while he needed her expert help.

"Let's see you get up on your own. Remember, Porter. No fast movements. Don't do anything that could jar you and set you back."

If she only knew what he'd been imagining. But Lily was right. He might think he could do what he wanted, but the only reason this was working was because he was concentrating on her instructions.

Before long he turned over and backed up to a kneeling position. Visualizing the final motion, he stood up and lowered himself into the wheelchair.

Lily bent over to undo the brake and adjust the feet. Then she lifted her head. "You've made wonderful progress. No severe tension lines in your face this afternoon. If you'll be this careful when you're taken home tomorrow, I don't see you having problems."

After she stood up, she walked over to the desk to make the phone call for the orderly. She never waited to give them a little more time to talk after their sessions. Lily Owens was professional beyond bearing at this point.

He followed her in the wheelchair. "My boss said he'd arrange for someone to come for me."

"I see on your orders that it will be Helen Jeffries, who's a licensed therapist. You'll like her. She's a wife and mother who does home visits, will stay overnight and drives patients to and from the clinic.

"A couple of my friends will be on hand to help."

"Even so, Helen will bring you here on Friday for your ten o'clock appointment with me and stay with you through the weekend." She paused. "Starting Monday you'll come to the clinic three times a week at the same time. We'll go from there and stay in touch with Mr. Fitzer."

"You're giving me VIP treatment."

"We try to give it to everyone, but I'll admit he thinks highly of you."

Porter took a deep breath. "Whom do I tell that I think highly of you? Dr. Jensen already knows how I feel. Is there someone higher up?"

She let out a gentle laugh. "You'll receive a form from the hospital you can fill out. I appreciate the compliment."

"Would it be out of line to tell you I like your new haircut?"

"Thanks. With summer here, a shorter hairdo feels good."

Just then Ron walked in and interrupted their conversation, causing Porter to moan inwardly. Like clockwork she retreated to her safe place. He was dying to know where she went after work, how she spent her time. Did she have a man admirer whom she might want to be with? So far Porter could think of four, including himself, who'd kill to be that person.

"Good luck going home tomorrow, Porter. Helen will have a list of instructions and numbers for you in case there's an emergency and you need to reach me, Dr. Jensen, or your regular doctor."

"That's good to know." He eyed Ron, letting him know he was ready to go.

"See you on Friday," she called out as he was wheeled into the hall.

Patience, Ewing.

That was the medicine he was forced to take if he hoped to initiate a personal relationship with her. As far as he could tell, she wasn't going anywhere, and certainly not without him.

Chapter 4

On Thursday morning, Lily took care of an emergency that had come in because she was free during the ten-o'clock hour. For the first three days of this week she'd taken care of the handsome ranger. It felt strange that she wouldn't be seeing him today, almost unnatural.

That's what alarmed her. Throughout her university training, the students in her classes had been warned about growing too attached to a patient. The ability to remain objective while giving care was very important, but unfortunately that wasn't always achievable. And in Porter Ewing's case, it was *impossible*.

The day he'd been wheeled in to her office, all her training went out the window. She was a total mess and had been ever since.

Relieved to have made plans with Millie, she drove

over to Style Clips on her lunch hour. They'd planned to go out for a bite to eat—Lily's treat. When she phoned her, Millie came out of the salon and got in her car.

She looked at Lily. "Your new hairstyle is perfect for a convertible."

Lily laughed. "I know. I love it. You did a wonderful job."

"Thanks, but the point is, how did the ranger react when he saw you yesterday?"

"He made a nice comment about it before he was wheeled away."

"*How* nice?"

"Just that he liked my new haircut. That's all."

Millie smiled at her. "Have you seen him this morning?"

She shook her head. "Not until tomorrow. I'm assuming he's home by now. Since he's been released from the hospital, he'll have to be driven to the clinic for therapy. If all goes well, he'll be able to drive his own car next week."

Lily took them to a new drive-thru that specialized in sandwiches and shakes. Since they both had to get back to work, they couldn't take the time to go to a restaurant.

"Jessica came in to the salon this morning to talk to her mom and ask her to tend her son Chase. It came up that the sheriff and some other friends were doing a surprise dinner for a good friend. She mentioned that his friend was just home from the hospital. Jessica could only have meant your ranger."

"He's not my ranger," she muttered. However, Lily

had to admit that she was glad that Porter had friends to help him get through this period.

"Are you sure you won't let me to talk to Jessica? Maybe she can find out something about him through her husband without giving anything away."

"Positive! The last thing I want is for him to think I'm interested in him."

A smile played on Millie's lips. "Even if you are."

"Yes."

"I know you're afraid."

"I could lose my job for fraternizing with a patient," she said.

"Come on, Lily. That hasn't stopped your boss from asking you out, to no avail. We both know why you're really nervous."

Their food was ready. Lily handed her everything and drove to the parking area, where they could eat.

"You're right. Steve lied to me in the most painful way possible. Thank heaven my teammate told me the truth before it was too late. That killed my love for him." She sighed. "But I hope I haven't lost the capacity to trust. Probably nothing will come of having met Porter. It's ridiculous to speculate. But thank you for being such a great friend."

"Ditto. Subject closed."

Lily drove them back to the salon to drop off Millie. "After work, I'm going to buy invitations for the shower and get them sent out. If you can think of anyone else you want to invite, let me know."

"Will do. You're a doll for doing all this for me, Lily."

"It's my absolute pleasure." She smiled warmly at

her friend. "Take care, Millie, and don't work too hard. Aren't you supposed to be putting your feet up?"

"I do when I get home. Talk to you soon. Thanks for lunch."

After Millie went inside, Lily drove back to the clinic. When she walked inside, Cindy called to her. "You have a couple of phone messages." She handed them to Lily.

"Thank you."

Once in her own office, she sat down at the desk to see who'd called her. The first one was from Brody's mother. The teen was still sick and wouldn't be able to come in until next week.

The second message shocked her. *Call Ranger Ewing.* Cindy had written the phone number.

Quickly, before her next patient showed up, she picked up the receiver of her office phone and pushed the digits, but her fingers were trembling.

"Ranger Ewing's residence." A woman answered, pulling the air out of Lily's lungs. She recognized the voice.

"Helen?"

"Hi, Lily. I'm so glad it's you."

"Is our patient all right?"

"He seems to be. I helped him into bed and have given him his lunch. Now I'm in the living room. A few minutes ago the phone rang. It was one of his friends. A bunch of them are coming over this evening to bring dinner and he told me I didn't have to stay overnight."

Lily's hand tightened on the receiver as she listened intently to what the home-care aide had to say. "Mr.

Porter insists he'll be fine and says I can leave now." She lowered her voice to a whisper. "He's being very forceful about it. But my job is to be here. You have the final say in this, Lily."

"Does he have a phone extension in the bedroom?"

"Yes," Helen answered.

"Tell him to get on the line and I'll talk to him."

"Thank you!" The other woman sounded relieved.

"Lily?" It was the sound of a familiar male voice. She swallowed hard.

"Hi, Porter. I gather you're home safe and sound and are already going crazy. Can I ask you a favor?"

"What do you think?" he asked in that deep, masculine tone that caused her heart to skip a beat.

"Helen would like to keep her job. Will you allow her to remain with you through tomorrow morning when you come for your therapy? She'll stay out of your way during the party that I understand your friends have planned for you."

"Is a party against the rules?"

"Of course not, but when you arrive at the clinic tomorrow, I'll arrange for you to talk to my boss. He'll have the final say on your treatment from here on out and clear it with your boss."

There was a moment of quiet before he said, "I didn't expect her to bother you or upset you. I'm sorry."

"No problem, but it's safe to say she hasn't had a patient who worked for the forest service before. You guys are a little more self-sufficient and independent than other folks."

"How come *you* can handle it?"

"I've lived around a father all my life who's tough as nails. So was my grandfather. You couldn't tell him anything. When he fell off the roof repairing some shingles and fractured a bone in his ankle, he got right up on the ladder the next day to finish the job. His doctor almost had a coronary."

That rich chuckle she loved rumbled out of him. "You've made your point. I'll behave. Since I still have you on the phone, why don't you drop by the ranch around six thirty and join the party? Helen will probably be happy for the company. Between the two of you, I should be well-guarded."

Her breath caught. Only an hour ago she'd told Millie that probably nothing would come of her meeting Porter. She gripped the receiver tighter. Seeing him off duty went against her own rules of self-preservation.

"As you should know, attending a patient's party is out of my job description, but thank you for the invitation. I hope you have a fun time, but please be careful so you don't undo all the progress you've made." She released a breath. "Tell Helen to call me anytime. Have a great day, Porter, and remember—no sudden moves!"

On that note she clicked off, still incredulous he'd invited her over to his house for a party.

"Lily? Is it all right to come in now?"

She wheeled around. "Madge—I didn't know you'd been standing there." The golfer who'd lost her husband had thrown out her back and needed therapy.

"I wasn't sure it was you at first. I thought you heard me knock."

"I'm sorry. Please come in."

The older woman smiled. "You look fantastic in that new hairstyle."

"Thank you."

"When did that happen?"

"Yesterday."

She shook her head with its titian-colored tint. "I can only imagine the number of car accidents you caused on the way to work."

"You're hilarious, Madge. Come on over to the mat and we'll get started."

"You know you look different? I'm not just talking about your hair."

"What do you mean?" Lily asked curiously.

"I'm pretty sure a man has something to do with it."

She rolled her eyes. "Why do women always say that?"

"Because it's often true! That's my thinking, anyway. Even after the death of my husband, not a day goes by without me thinking of him."

"Madge…" She was handling her loss so well.

"You know what I'm talking about."

The examining room rang with Lily's laughter. "You're like a burst of fresh air, Madge."

"Happy twenty-eighth birthday, Porter!"

The guys and their wives had learned he'd turned a year older today and had used his first evening home from the hospital to celebrate with great food and a cake. He thanked his buddies for the new leather gloves they'd given him as a gift for when he drove his truck.

While everyone did the cleanup, with Mrs. Jeffries

in charge, Holden walked over and sat next to him in the living room so they could talk privately. The therapist had helped Porter into an overstuffed chair that felt good on his back.

"I wanted to ask you about the perp who ran away from you the night of your accident. Give me the sequence of events."

Porter thought for a minute. "I made him hand over his rifle before I searched him and his gear, but after my horse fell on top of me and the rifle, I couldn't stop him from disappearing. He could have tried to get the rifle out from under me, but for some reason he didn't. I'm not sure why he didn't finish me off unless he worried the other ranger in the fire tower was looking for me."

"Thank goodness! We'll find him. In your report you wrote 'Jake Harrison from Big Piney, Wyoming,' and that he works for the railroad."

"That's what he told me."

"I put your information through the database, but nothing came up. Every answer was a lie. No one has ever heard of him. Tell me what you remember about him."

"He had no ID on him and was in his mid-twenties, maybe five feet nine, thin, overly long dark hair, a full beard and surly temperament. He wore a denim jacket and jeans that could have been bought anywhere."

Holden nodded. "Stan ordered the rifle brought in and taken to forensics. We're trying to find out if he stole it or bought it somewhere in the state."

"That's good. I was surprised he'd been brazen enough to light a fire and hunt without a permit when both aren't allowed. He had no horse. My first thought was that he's on the run and not up there to hunt at all. He had no way to carry out any game. It didn't make sense. I'm thinking he had a contact."

"I agree." The sheriff pressed his lips into a grim line. "Hopefully Cyril will get some fingerprints that will help us find out who he is and if there are outstanding warrants for his arrest."

"I'm glad you're looking into it, Holden. I plan to be back on the job soon. Thanks again for the party."

"It was our pleasure. We're gonna clear out now so you can get some sleep."

Before long Porter's house had emptied. He was aware of an ache that was especially strong tonight after being with his friends. They made marriage look good. The absence of a woman in his life was starting to wear on him, but the thought of getting married to the wrong woman still gave him pause.

Part of him had been hoping Lily might just decide to drop in, anyway. But she kept herself aloof. No doubt there was a reason. Every workplace had rules about the employees mingling with the clients, but he didn't believe that was what held her back from being more forthcoming. Porter didn't mind having to wait until tomorrow, because he would be seeing her again.

Helen drove Porter to the hospital the following morning for his ten-o'clock appointment. Ron met them at the hospital entrance with a wheelchair. Helen said she'd be here after his workout to drive him back to his house.

After not seeing Lily all day yesterday, his excitement grew as he was rolled down the hall to the therapy room. The door was open, but there was no sign of her.

"She'll be here shortly."

"Go ahead and leave me, Ron."

"Can't do that."

After a two-minute wait, Lily breezed in bringing her delicious flowery scent with her. "Sorry I'm late, Porter. I was in on a consultation with Dr. Jensen. Thanks, Ron."

"You bet. See you later."

Porter took inventory of her face and figure. Today she was wearing a hot pink top and tan boot-cut chino pants beneath her lab coat.

"Why don't you wheel yourself over to my desk. I want to discuss something with you before we start your workout."

The tone of her voice didn't indicate something was wrong, but he couldn't help but be curious as to where this was leading. He followed her and waited until she'd sat down. Her exquisite eyes met his.

"You look free of pain today."

"For the most part I am. My cheek still hurts."

She nodded. "I imagine the party made you want to get back into the fray."

"You have no idea."

"Oh, I think I do." Her smile nearly gave him a heart attack. "After talking to you and your boss, I'm aware you're going crazy from inactivity. I also realize you're a man without a horse. Since I know that you do most of your ranger duties on the back of one, it's essential we get you in the saddle again soon."

He pursed his lips.

"I saw that," she claimed. "The thought of getting on one has to make you cringe, but I'm not talking about the Arabians, like the ones the forest service provides."

"Are you saying there's a special kind of horse for someone like me?"

"That's exactly what I'm saying," she replied.

"I'm all ears."

"Have you ever heard of a Missouri Fox Trotter?"

Porter nodded. "My friend Cole wouldn't ride another breed. He says Samson is the most sure-footed animal he's ever ridden."

"He'd be right," she concurred. "Trotters are not only noted for being sure-footed, they're *especially* sought-after for the disabled because of their smooth ride."

"You're kidding!"

"No. They give those people who've injured their backs gentler movement."

His eyes lit with interest. "How does that work?"

"The gaited breed is known for its stamina and smooth gait. It performs an ambling gait nicknamed the 'fox-trot,' because of its broken diagonal gait. That's when the front feet of the diagonal pair lands before the hind. The result eliminates that moment of suspension and increases smoothness."

"Wow. I had no idea."

"You won't appreciate the difference until you ride on one," she told him. "I wasn't convinced, either, not with my injured spine. Then my therapist put me on a

Trotter. I couldn't believe how comfortable I felt riding one. It was incredible."

"Was this when you were in Salt Lake City?"

"Yes. The clinic there had access to a rancher who raised Trotters."

"Do you ride one now?" he asked.

"Absolutely. I swear by them. While a segment of my patients who ride horses are healing, I put them on the back of a Trotter to help ease them back into activity."

"Where do you do that?"

"At my parents' ranch here in Whitebark. Three months ago when I came back here to live and started in this position, my parents got into the Missouri Fox Trotter business. They now raise them and allow me to bring some of my patients to the ranch for their horse therapy." She flashed him a grin. "See? I told you they're saints."

Porter was even more impressed by their devotion to their daughter. "That's because they believe in you, Lily. Does this mean you ride with your patients?"

She nodded. "I'm telling you about it now because your boss wants to get you another horse, possibly an Arabian. Apparently most of the rangers use them. But because of your injury, I suggest you try a Trotter first to see how you feel." She hesitated. "There's no hurry. Only when you feel comfortable enough to get on a horse again. Depending on how you move, maybe for your Friday appointment next week."

A whole week away... "I'll talk it over with my boss."

"Good. Are you ready for another workout?"

She had no idea how motivated he was to improve so he could go riding with her on her family's ranch. He wheeled himself over to the pad without any prompting and took his time getting down the way she'd taught him. So far there'd been none of those sharp pains she'd talked about on that first day. After he rolled over, he smiled up at her. "Do you still think I'm a fraud?"

"I don't know. I'm still working on it."

He frowned. "Why do I get the feeling you have reservations about me?"

Her cheeks reddened, whether in embarrassment or anger, he didn't know. "You're my patient. I don't have any feelings about you except to see you get better."

"I'm doing my hardest."

"I know you are so you can go after that horrible man who disappeared on you in the mountains. Okay, let's get started."

On Saturday Lily did some shopping for the upcoming baby shower before driving to Jackson Hole to attend a yearly physiotherapist conference. After sleeping in on Sunday, she rode her horse and helped her parents with the other horses. She told them about Porter, and that he was from Lake Placid, New York, and his desire to get back on a horse. Her folks suggested she let him ride Dash to see if it worked for him.

They talked about various horses and she ended up telling them about what had happened to him near the Crow's Nest. But the realization that she was talking about him too much, and waiting to see him, angered her. She didn't want to be hung up on a man again, not when she'd been going along fine for the last eight years without one in her life.

When Lily got ready for work Monday morning, she felt out of sorts. Nothing in her wardrobe appealed. She should have bought some more tops on Saturday, but she'd refused to spend money since her uniform covered her up. In the end she chose jeans and a khaki blouse he hadn't seen. Not that Porter would notice.

She couldn't put him out of her mind while she did her makeup and brushed her hair into the style that had brought her compliment after compliment. All Porter had said was that he liked it. But that didn't help her.

Determined to fight her attraction, she entered her office and focused on her eight-thirty patient, Domingo Salazar, a local bowling sensation. He'd thrown out his back during a recent workout and needed therapy before a big tournament next month. The married man with two children was a fun-loving chap.

After the workout he turned to her. "I feel better already and have two free tickets for the bowling tournament next month in Casper. They're yours for helping me." He left them on the corner of her desk before walking out just as Ron wheeled Porter in.

"Thanks, Domingo!" she called after him. That was kind of him.

Her eyes fell on Porter, whose intense gaze enveloped her, raising her pulse rate to a dangerous level.

"Good morning, Lily." His deep voice penetrated her body. "How was your weekend?"

"Fine. How was yours? Did Helen take good care of you?"

"She's great… I have no complaints," he replied.

"After my session here, she'll drive me to headquarters. My boss has plans to keep me busy this week."

"But not all day every day." She finished washing her hands.

"Why not? I feel good."

"That's what worries me, Porter. If you don't take regular breaks, your pain will come back. You'll have to establish a balance. Now, I want to work with you on the side stepladder table. Wheel yourself over here."

She waited until he did her bidding before kneeling down to fix the wheelchair feet and remove his slippers. "I'm glad Helen has put nonslip socks on you."

"I feel like a baby. All I need is a bonnet."

Lily chuckled. "Do you know my father once dressed up for a Halloween party like a baby? Mother carried his bottle. All he wore was a diaper and bonnet. I almost died laughing when I saw him."

Porter's eyes twinkled. "You'll never catch me doing that, except for these slippers, of course."

"You'd be quite a sight I'm sure. Okay. Visualize what you're going to do. Stand up and put your hands on the table while you get up on the stepladder. Easy does it." She glanced over at him to check his progress. "Now extend one arm and get in a kneeling position. Once you're comfortable, turn on your back. At first it'll feel a little strange being up from the floor. Move slowly."

He minded her. If it bothered him, he didn't show it. She worked with his legs for the next twenty minutes, then showed him how to get up in a sitting position before lowering himself to the floor and back in the wheelchair.

"I've been watching for tension lines, Porter, and am pleased to say that I don't see any. Your pain ratio is way down."

He nodded. "That's thanks to you since I've been taking your advice. Do you think I could take a ride on a Trotter on Wednesday instead of Friday? I discussed it with my boss and he's all for it since he needs more rangers than he's got covering the mountains in summer."

"That's understandable, of course, but it might be pushing you a little too much." She furrowed her brow. "Let's see how well you do on Wednesday afternoon for your therapy. If all looks right, maybe we could arrange for an early evening ride at the ranch, provided Helen can drive you to and from."

"I'll ask her in a few minutes."

"Look, Porter. I know you're anxious to get back to work, but I'm cautioning you to take this in increments for your overall health."

He nodded. "I know that, and I won't do anything stupid if I don't feel I'm ready."

"Then that's good enough for me." She put his slippers on him and fixed the feet of the wheelchair before walking over to her desk. Porter followed. As she reached for the mouse on her computer the tickets fell. "Oh—"

He looked down. "I would pick them up, but I just promised you no sudden movements."

"I'm glad you said that." She retrieved them, hoping Mr. Salazar would improve enough for him to compete. "My last patient left them."

"Do you like bowling?" Porter had seen the printing on the tickets.

"Not really. The few times I tried, the ball ended up in the alley."

His smile robbed her of breath. "That makes two of us."

To her relief, the familiar knock on the door interrupted their conversation. "Come on in, Ron! My patient is ready to leave."

She'd said it deliberately to remind herself that their session was over. Yet her disappointment that he was leaving filled her with a troubling sense of loss.

Lily didn't want to miss his company, but something uncanny had been happening to her. Porter was growing on her by the minute. If they started riding together, that could compound the ache for him that was growing inside of her.

"See you Wednesday, Lily." Porter's parting words jerked her back to her surroundings.

"You bet. Same time. Same place," she said over her shoulder without meeting his eyes.

Maybe she *would* ask for Millie's help. Maybe her friend could find out something about Porter through Jessica that would be a real turnoff. Because right now, Lily couldn't stop thinking about him.

Thank goodness Monday turned out to be a busy one. She'd succeeded in pushing Porter to the back of her mind until she had a phone call from Helen late in the day.

"Hi, Lily. Just checking in. I took Mr. Ewing home

from work. He's been careful and seems to be doing fine. He told me he plans to go horseback riding on Wednesday evening on your say-so."

Lily bit down on her lip. "What do *you* think?"

"Like I said, he moves well and insists he's not experiencing new pain."

"That's good to know." She released a breath. "When he comes in on Wednesday afternoon, I'll ask Dr. Jensen to take a look at him and see if he's ready. With three of us making the decision, I'll feel better about it."

"Between you and me, he's a real hunk."

Yup. "Better not tell Wayne that."

Helen laughed. "Don't worry. There are secrets, and then there are secrets I *keep* from my hubby."

Amen.

Lily'd had all day to think about Porter despite trying desperately not to. He was a New Yorker. It didn't make sense why he'd left an established career in a fabulous area of the country like Lake Placid to come out to Wyoming. During the Olympics she'd been blindsided by Steve and wouldn't be making that mistake again.

What secret are you running away from, Porter?

Chapter 5

Wednesday afternoon Helen arrived at the ranch and drove Porter to his therapy session. Ron met them outside the physiotherapy clinic entrance with the wheelchair. Porter didn't need it anymore, but it was hospital rules.

"What's going on?" he asked when Ron deposited him in front of Dr. Jensen's door.

"I don't know. I was asked to bring you here." He knocked on the door. Within seconds Dr. Jensen appeared.

"Good afternoon, Ranger Ewing. Come in and let's see how much progress you've made."

Porter had been living to see Lily. This was a blow he hadn't seen coming. "Couldn't my therapist be here?"

"She'll join us at the end of our session."

Damn.

The doctor had him get up on the side stepladder table and go through similar exercises Lily had performed on Monday. When it was over, he got back in the wheelchair while the doctor made a call. In another minute Lily entered, in her lab coat, more beautiful than a woman had the right to be. He noticed the doctor couldn't take his eyes off her, either.

She flashed Porter the kind of smile he imagined she gave all her patients. Nothing personal. "Good morning. How's that back today?"

It wasn't his back bothering him anymore, but all he said was "Fine."

Dr. Jensen concurred, then nodded before looking at Porter. "You're moving well, but I think you should wait until Friday to get on a horse for the first time." So that meant Lily had already talked to the doctor about it. "I'd advise another forty-eight hours to give the body more time to heal. It's better to err on the side of caution."

"I couldn't agree more," she said, even though Porter knew she was aware that he couldn't handle this inertia much longer. "Under the circumstances, I'll see you at the ranch at six o'clock on Friday. Helen knows the address."

Hallelujah!

"No cowboy boots, just regular shoes. Have a wonderful day, Porter. Talk to you later, Matt."

As she walked out of the therapy room, Ron came in. Porter glanced at the doctor. "Thank you for your help."

"Not at all. That's what we're here for."

Tamping down his excitement that he'd be riding

with her the day after tomorrow, he couldn't be happier as Helen drove him to work and walked him into the office where he'd been working. She'd made him sandwiches for his dinner because he'd be there late.

"I'll be back to take you home when you call me."

"Thanks for everything, Helen." If all went well after his horseback ride on Friday, he'd drive himself to work in his own car starting Monday.

Stan had given him a ton of paperwork to do. Around quitting time for everyone else, Holden came in with milk shakes for both of them.

"Thanks. You're a sight for sore eyes. Sit down and share my dinner with me, compliments of my aide. I'm working late."

"Don't mind if I do."

Porter opened the sack and pulled out the sandwiches and chips for both of them. "I hope you have some news on that culprit."

Holden frowned. "Don't I wish. When Cyril gave me the results, I ran the fingerprints from the rifle through the database. No match. That's what has me bothered." He scrubbed a hand across his jaw. "I've put out an APB on him here and in the surrounding states. A couple of my men went up to the spot where he'd made the fire, looking for any evidence. And you know what really puzzles me?"

"No—what?" Porter asked.

"Why didn't he go after the other ranger at the fire tower?"

Porter shook his head. "Maybe he never got near the lookout. Did your men turn up any other evidence?"

"Not right there, but they did find some stubs of cigarettes closer to the fire lookout. They brought them back to the lab. It's the old needle-in-the-haystack problem. They might be leaked to the culprit if we catch him.

"We've learned the butts were only a week or two old, and we have saliva samples to provide DNA. All the butts came from the same person. It turns out they were Captain Black cigarillos, not something most people smoke here in Wyoming."

Porter blinked. "I *know* that brand."

"I've never seen you smoke."

"I don't, but when I was back in New York, I worked with a female ranger who planned to buy some Captain Black cigarillos for her brother for Christmas. Odd how that memory has stuck with me."

Holden leaned back in his chair. "Not odd if she was the special woman in your life you can't forget." His dark eyebrows lifted. "Is she the reason you're still single? I don't mean to pry, but I *have* wondered. Anytime you want to talk about it, I'm available."

No one had a better friend than Porter did in Holden. "I know you've had questions. How much time do you have?"

"I'm off duty and we're alone."

Porter looked around, realizing there'd never be a better moment. "I'll start at the beginning. A year before I was transferred out here, there was a female ranger with the forest service in the Adirondacks.

"She'd been working three years in other regions, but because of problems with her male coworkers I was never told about, she'd been transferred to various units before coming to mine in the Adirondacks High Peaks."

"What time period was that?" Holden asked.

"Let me think. I've been out here in Wyoming a year. She'd been assigned to my unit in November prior to my leaving New York the next June, so I knew her about six months in all."

"What was her name?"

"Melissa Reiver," Porter replied. "She was a good-looking woman, maybe five foot three, long dark hair, brown eyes, an expert marksman." A shiver of revulsion shot down Porter's back when he thought about what she'd done to him.

"That's it?" He smiled. "Come on, man, you can't leave me hanging."

Porter sucked in his breath. It was time to tell his friend why Porter had been immediately hired by the forest service here in Wyoming.

"What I'm about to reveal is something no else knows about except for my boss, Stan. There's a reason I've kept the details of my arrival in Wyoming a secret from everyone, even from you and the guys. You see, my former boss, Martin Kroger, put my case under seal for everyone's protection, particularly mine."

"Case?" Holden's smile faded and he studied him hard. "This sounds serious."

"Very." He took a deep breath. "You want to know the reason why I'm here? From the moment she arrived, Melissa did everything but stand on her head to get my attention. I had to train her for the first month, but her desire to be alone with me became so obvious,

I was suspicious. I knew there was something wrong with her from the start."

He hesitated for a moment. "I'm afraid it's a long story."

"I'm listening. Go on."

"I kept avoiding her the best I could. Finally, I put in a transfer application in order to get away from her without pointing to her as the reason. In the meantime, I had to keep doing my job waiting for my transfer to go through.

"One night in January, there were three of us snowed in. Ranger Archuleta, a good man, had already gone to his pup tent. We each had one. Melissa used the excuse that she was frightened so I'd sleep in her tent with her."

"You've got to be kidding me!" Holden exclaimed.

"Nope. I knew what she was trying to do and had it out with her. I told her that she should get assigned to another sector ASAP or I'd report her. She shouted several profanities at me before crawling in her tent alone. To my relief, the next thing I knew she was gone from my area."

"Thank heaven."

"I didn't hear about her again until my boss Martin told me to come in to headquarters. I thought it was about my transfer request and I planned to tell him I'd changed my mind.

"To my shock he asked me if I'd had relations with Ranger Reiver the night of the snowstorm. You can imagine my reaction."

Holden nodded. "I know I would have exploded."

"I almost did. I let him know under no uncertain

terms how uninterested I'd ever been in her. Of course, I knew the rules against employees getting involved and I would never have broken them. Anything like that was grounds for dismissal.

"Martin looked at me for a long moment and said, 'Ranger Reiver came to my office yesterday claiming she's pregnant with your baby.'"

"Holy hell—" Holden blurted.

"She told Martin that her doctor had said she'd have to go on maternity leave by August at the latest and she was giving me a chance to own up to my responsibility."

Holden just sat there, shaking his head.

"Of course, I denied everything. I knew it couldn't be my baby, but if there was one, a paternity test would prove I wasn't the father."

"Did you have to take the test?"

"No. Thank God, Martin believed me, but asked if I knew of a compelling reason why Melissa wanted to get me into that kind of trouble. I had to conclude that this was her revenge on me for rejecting her. She had to know it would put me in the worst possible light and could cost me my job. At that point I told Martin I believed she was seriously unstable.

"He agreed and said he now understood why I'd put in a transfer several months earlier, but he chastised me for not reporting her behavior at that time."

Holden nodded in agreement. "You should have, Porter."

"I realize that now, but I didn't like doing that to her if I didn't have to."

"In your case trying to be a gentleman didn't help you," his friend reminded him.

A muscle ticked in Porter's jaw. "You're not kidding. To my everlasting gratitude, Martin arranged with Stan to transfer me here to Wyoming, far from her reach. I flew out here the next day."

"That was lucky for us."

"For me, too," Porter said. "Martin started an investigation and kept me informed."

"Did he dig up any dirt?"

"Heck yeah. He discovered that for the three years Melissa had worked for the forest service prior to coming to the High Peaks, she'd been transferred four times for hitting on some of her male coworkers in order to be alone with them. That told us both she'd exhibited a pattern of disturbing behavior that had gone on for years."

"Well, as you said, something was clearly very wrong with that woman," Holden said.

"Last August he phoned to tell me the results of the official inquiry. They proved she wasn't pregnant and had been lying the whole time she'd been with the forest service. The powers that be fired her without the chance of being hired again, and they stripped her of her pension because of the seriousness of the charges."

"Well, at least she got what was coming to her."

"I suppose, but the damage had already been done," he said. "She'd lied under oath and caused me to leave a job I loved with the forest service." He slanted a glance the other man's way. "So now you know the whole sordid story of the 'special woman' in my life. Ranger

Reiver wasn't only unstable and vindictive, she was dangerous."

Holden let out a whistle. "She could very well be behind what happened to you here in order to carry out her revenge."

Porter took a deep breath. "I suppose it's possible."

"I need to talk to your Commissioner Kroger and ask him to send me a photo of her to be distributed."

"He'll cooperate, but it seems a stretch, Holden. It happened in another part of the country and was a long time ago."

"Not that long, Porter," he said solemnly. "Remember Jessica's story? The man who was ultimately responsible for her husband's death was biding his time waiting for her since high school. Even after his death, the lowlife didn't make his move until recently and had been planning her kidnapping. When they go mental like that, there's no telling what they're capable of."

Porter hissed out a breath. "You're right. There was something strange about Melissa from the start."

"This culprit could be a hired gun for her."

"Maybe he's a boyfriend," he interjected, "but I don't see how she could know I'm here, of all places."

Holden leaned forward. "Tell me what happened after you left Martin's office that morning. Go step by step." Holden wasn't a great detective for nothing.

"His assistant, Ranger Michael Denny, drove me and my rig to a car rental in Lake Placid and dropped me off. I drove to the family home. My mother had rented it, and I went over there in order to get some of my belongings from the basement. I was there about an hour, then I drove to the airport in New York that very day and dropped off the rental car."

Holden's eyes gleamed with interest. "Do you think Melissa had been hanging around afterward, stalking you? Maybe she saw you at headquarters. Do you think she might have questioned the ranger who drove you to Lake Placid? Or is it possible she followed you there?"

"I guess anything could have happened."

Holden grimaced. "I want to talk to Ranger Denny as well as Martin. Her fury must have been severe when she discovered you'd disappeared from sight within a day. No doubt her fantasies had included marrying you and having your child. It's been a year since you left. Since her firing and loss of pension, she could have been making other kinds of plans for you."

"I don't doubt that, but if there is a connection to her and the culprit here, I'm still amazed she could have found out where I was sent. The commissioner put everyone in his employ under strict orders to say nothing about me or they'd be fired."

"Did Melissa know where you lived in New York?" Holden asked.

"I never had conversations like that with her," he replied. "However, a lot of people knew the Ewing home was in Lake Placid because my father was a legend around there. He'd worked for the forest service for years before I joined."

"But you said you sold the home in order to buy your ranch here."

"Yes, but not for a few months."

"Maybe she tracked you to Lake Placid hoping to

find you home and ended up talking to the renters." Holden leaned back in his seat, and laced his fingers behind his head. "What information did they have on you?"

Porter let out a sound of self-disgust. "I was in such a hurry and so angry, I wasn't thinking except to get away as soon as possible. Before I left in the rental car, I wrote down my new address of the barracks here in Whitebark and asked them to ship the rest of my belongings."

Holden nodded. "If she did approach them, then they would probably have told her what she wanted to know, thinking she was your girlfriend or something."

Hell.

"What are the names of the renters?"

"The Elkins. They moved out when the house was sold. I don't know where they live now, but I can find out."

"We'll locate them if you give me all the information you've got on them," Holden said.

"I've papers at the ranch and will fax them to you the second I get home."

"Sounds good," he murmured. "And as soon as the commissioner sends me a photo of her, I'd like to send it to the renters and have a talk. Let's hope they can tell us if a woman under an assumed name or disguise who resembled her came looking for you wanting a forwarding address. It's worth pursuing."

"I couldn't agree more," Porter agreed. "When I look back on it, I wouldn't put anything past that woman. If she was that bent on destroying me, she could definitely have talked to them, then hired someone to come looking for me wanting revenge when I least expected it." He exhaled roughly. "So far you've gotten no feedback from the criminal data base after testing the cigarette butts?"

"That's correct. But the second I know, I'll tell you."

One recurring thought nagged at Porter. "When Melissa told me about wanting to buy those cigarillos for her brother, I didn't know she even had one and—"

"Porter—" Holden said, cutting him off. "Maybe the culprit *is* her brother."

He stared at the other man. "I suppose it's possible, but there have to be thousands of people who buy that brand."

"Well, I'm going to find out! I'm running those prints through the database again, but this time I'll add the name *Reiver* and see what comes up."

"That's a long shot," Porter said.

"It's usually the one that works." He finished off his shake. "How soon before you're back in the saddle?"

For the next few minutes Porter told him what would be happening.

"A Trotter, huh?"

"Yup. I'm going to try one and see how it feels."

"Why not? Cole's a convert." He collected his trash and got to his feet. "I wish you luck, buddy, and thanks for the sandwich. Now I'd better get home and let you get back to work."

Porter flashed him a smile. "Thanks for the company and the shake. When I get a clean bill of health, I'll be helping you on the manhunt if that deadbeat still hasn't been caught." That day couldn't come soon enough for several reasons.

"I'm counting on it."

Porter kept busy in the office and managed to fill his time until late Friday afternoon, when Helen picked him up from headquarters. Being careful, he climbed in front with her and they left for the Owens ranch, three miles away.

"Lily says you've been out there before."

"A few times to deliver and pick up patients. If you think she's a great therapist, you haven't seen anything until you see her helping folks get back in the saddle again. She's an expert equestrian."

"That doesn't surprise me." He recalled Lily telling him that her grandmother had taught her how to ride. She'd also divulged that her grandfather had been a big hunter.

Soon they came to the entrance with a sign hanging below the antler archway. *Owens Ranch. Missouri Fox Trotters sold here.*

His gaze went to the idyllic two-story ranch house set back in the trees, with a well-kept lawn and flowers. Helen drove them past the tree-lined drive of elms and poplars to the rear of the house. From there it opened up to a cluster of outbuildings and equipment, a barn, a covered corral and two other open corrals, all in per-fect condition.

Helen wound around farther to a grassy paddock, where he saw Lily in a white Stetson holding the reins of two saddled Trotters. His focus on her blotted everything else from his mind.

He'd never seen her without her lab coat. This evening she wore jeans with cowboy boots and a tan Western shirt with fringe. The shape of her curvaceous body took his breath away.

"Porter? Are you all right?" Helen had come around to help him out of the car.

"Yes. I was just looking at the…chestnut she's holding. That's a beautiful horse." For that matter, so was the pinto. Not until then did he notice a wooden three-legged stool placed next to the chestnut. Porter grimaced. He really was a baby to need that to get on a horse, but would go along with it this once.

Helen stood by as he got out of the car the way she'd shown him. "Thanks for the ride."

"I'll be back in an hour." He heard her shut the door.

Much as he wanted to tell her to show up much later, he held back and walked carefully toward Lily. She glanced at him beneath the brim of her cowboy hat. "Right on time, Ranger, and proceeding with caution I see."

"I've been counting the minutes until I could get back on a horse."

"I know that. So come on over and meet Dash."

Porter chuckled. "I like the name."

"I've told him all about you. He's a four-year-old gelding who's eager to belong to someone who really knows how to ride. Out of all our horses, Dash would be the perfect fit for you in size and temperament. He loves the mountains and has the sweetest disposition under pressure."

He walked over to the pinto first and patted her hind end. "What's this one's name?"

"Trixie. She's my mare. The best horse I ever owned." Lily smiled up at him. "It's nice to see you on your feet and walking almost normally. You weren't in the best shape when you were brought in to the hospital."

His lips twisted in amusement. "Tell me about it."

"Let's get you started. This isn't so different from climbing on the table. I'll hold the reins while you grip the pommel and get on the stool. Don't worry about Dash. He'll remain steady."

Her phenomenal faith in the chestnut horse gave him confidence and he did her bidding. The stool made all the difference to reduce the strain.

"Now put your left foot in the stirrup. When you're ready and have thought out the movement, carefully move your right leg to get in the saddle. I want to know if you feel any pain. All right?"

"Got it." After visualizing the motion, he took care as he lifted his leg and sat down in the saddle.

She looked up at him with concern in those gorgeous violet eyes. "What's the verdict?"

"I expected to feel pain, but it didn't come, only a twinge."

"Nothing worse?" she prodded.

He shook his head. "No. I'm fine now that I'm sitting."

"Then so far so good."

"After my accident that night in the mountains, I couldn't have imagined being on a horse again."

"You're making a marvelous recovery." She handed him the reins and moved the stool out of the way. Then she mounted her pinto in a fluid movement that revealed years of experience. "We'll simply ride around the paddock with no sudden turns. This will give Dash time to get used to you, too."

Porter made a clicking sound and released the tension on the reins. Dash automatically moved forward. Lily rode at his side and they walked their horses at a slow pace for about ten minutes. "Are you noticing any difference yet?"

He shot her a glance. "I'm shocked how smooth the ride is. You've already convinced me this horse lives up to all the things you've told me."

Lily nodded. "A Trotter can canter or do the gaited fox-trot like it's doing now. Because of its sliding glide, you could be comfortable for hours at a time. They're especially sure-footed in the mountains over rocks and roots where it's steep."

"How often has Dash been ridden?"

"Every day, either with the staff, my parents or myself. So far he hasn't sold because the buyers haven't been your height and weight. You're welcome to keep riding him until you feel a hundred percent and decide what kind of a horse you want."

They rode for another twenty minutes while she extolled the virtues of the breed. He felt no discomfort and his body relaxed in the saddle.

"How are you feeling now?"

"Like I could keep going for hours," he answered.

"I said the same thing to the therapist in Salt Lake City who took me riding for the first time. I couldn't believe I had no discomfort after what I'd lived through. In fact I'm embarrassed to admit I broke down for happiness. Even if I couldn't ski again, I could ride. That meant everything to me."

Glancing her way, he said gently, "I can only imagine. It's a shame what happened to you."

"It could have been worse. Now I have a different career because of it."

"One you do brilliantly," he reminded her. "Just so you know, I trust your judgment, Lily. Next week I'll ask my boss to take a ride on Dash to show him the difference. He owns an Arabian. If he has proof that this horse will help me do my job, he might be willing to make the purchase for me. That is if Dash is for sale."

"He is."

They started back. "After this ride, I'd be afraid to get on another breed in case it did damage."

She turned to him. "Promise me you won't try it. Not for at least another month."

He pulled to a stop. "What is your plan for me for next week?"

"The same as this one. Monday, Wednesday and Friday ten-o'clock sessions."

"And horseback rides in the evenings?" he asked hopefully.

"We can if you're feeling up to it."

She had no clue how ready he was to spend hours with her, but he knew he mustn't push it. "What about you? Your dedication to your patients doesn't give you much time to yourself."

A small laugh escaped her lips. "I like to stay busy. Last night I gave a baby shower for a friend. Last weekend I attended a conference in Jackson Hole."

"What about this weekend?"

"I ride with the Wind River Women's Brigade. We've been called on for all kinds of searches. This time we're on a hunt for a downed single-engine plane in the Bridger-Teton forest up by Glimpse Lake. The first shift went out yesterday. Tomorrow our second group will relieve them."

Porter was stunned. "I didn't know you belonged to that group. Do you stay out all night?"

"Usually."

An image of the culprit who'd made his escape the night of the accident flashed into his mind. He might still be out there somewhere. Was he involved with Melissa in some way? "That could be dangerous."

"We're well-trained and each of us carries a weapon, so it's not a problem."

He cleared his throat. "Lily, I'm going to tell you something I shouldn't, but I don't want you or your friends to get hurt."

"What are you talking about?"

"Just remember that hunter could be up there somewhere, so be careful. The sheriff has put out an APB on him. One of the reasons I want to get back to work is so I can go after him. There's been no sign of him."

"Do you think he's armed?"

"I kept his rifle, but he might have found himself

another weapon." He clenched his jaw. "That's what has me worried."

"You have my word I'll be careful," she told him. "Do you have a physical description of him? I can give it to our captain to make everyone aware."

Porter told her everything he could remember before he saw that Helen had arrived. The last thing he wanted to do was leave Lily. After he got home he'd phone her to make sure she understood how dangerous this situation could be.

He led Dash to the stool and followed Lily's instructions for dismounting. He felt a little stiff, but there was no pain. When he handed her the reins, he closed his hand over hers. "Thank you, Lily. Not just for this evening, but for everything. I'll see you on Monday."

He patted Dash's rump affectionately and took his time walking to the car, worried because Lily would be going into the mountains tomorrow. On the drive to his ranch with Helen, he broke out in a cold sweat.

If anything happened to Lily, it would destroy him.

Chapter 6

Marjorie Austin, the fifty-year-old captain of the women's brigade, faced them on her roan. Lily had already phoned their captain and told her what Porter had warned her about.

"Good morning, ladies! Welcome to Glimpse Lake. This is our rendezvous point. A word of warning first. A wanted fugitive could be hiding up here having nothing to do with the downed plane. We don't know if he's armed or not. He's in his mid-twenties, five feet nine, thin, overly long dark hair with a full beard and a surly nature.

"Take extreme caution and report anything unusual to me. You're all armed so I know you have protection. Now that you've been given a master grid, study it carefully to see where you and your partner are assigned."

"I'm glad we're paired together," Deedee whispered to Lily.

"Me, too."

Deedee was a barrel rider in the rodeo and engaged to be married. She'd been one of the girls at the baby shower for Millie. They'd all ridden together for years and enjoyed each other's company.

"Gals? The second you find anything, phone in to me. We'll all come together again at five thirty and set up our overnight camp. Let's pray we find that plane today. Off you go and good luck!"

The two of them headed toward their area where a number painted on a post indicated they were in the right spot to begin their part of the search in the heavily forested ground cover. They'd brought food and water in their backpacks. The day had turned out warm and beautiful, but Lily was sad to think a plane had gone down here and people had died.

After three hours of going back and forth on one side of the grid, they'd found no parts of a plane or anything else. By now they'd reached the ten-thousand-foot level near the Crow's Nest, where Porter had suffered the accident on his horse.

They dismounted to eat lunch. With him constantly on her mind, she walked over to Deedee while munching on a sandwich. "I have something important to tell you."

"That sounds serious."

"It has to do with the announcement Marjorie made to us about a fugitive. Yesterday one of my patients who's a ranger with the forest service was driven to the ranch to try out one of our Trotters for therapy."

"Is he cute?"

Great. Not Deedee, too.

"*Cute* doesn't accurately describe him, but that's not what's important."

Deedee finished off her own sandwich. "In other words, he's a hottie, right?"

"Deedee—" she cried in frustration.

"Oh, boy. You have it bad. Go on."

She took a drink from her water bottle. "I need to give you a little background. He turned up at the clinic after being thrown from his horse in the middle of the night right up here by the Crow's Nest. His horse broke a leg and had to be put down."

"Oh, no!"

"It had to have been horrible, but there's more." Lily told her the rest of the story.

"So that's the creep who got away from him and could still be out here?"

"It's possible," she confirmed. "The police haven't found him, not even with an APB out on him."

"He's probably armed."

"I agree. The ranger took away his rifle, but he could have other weapons. I told him if I saw someone matching his description, I'd phone him. That's why I told Marjorie."

Deedee nodded. "I've been keeping a lookout."

"I have, too. Hopefully he's not anywhere around."

"Are you ready to do the other side of our grid?" the other woman asked.

"Let's go. What a shame we haven't found any evidence of the plane to help those grieving families."

"Maybe we still will."

They walked back to their horses and mounted. Within ten minutes they came across signs of a small campfire that had been abandoned. "Stop for a minute, Deedee. Maybe this is the place where Porter tangled with that lowlife."

She shot Lily a smile. "It's Porter now, huh?" she teased.

"Will you give it up?" But she chuckled as she said it before riding Trixie around.

When she didn't see anything out of the ordinary, they kept moving through the dense forest. "We need to be careful our horses don't step in that woodchuck burrow. It's around here somewhere."

After five minutes they came across evidence that someone had built another small fire. Deedee shook her head. "What gives with people lighting fires in a no-fire zone?"

"It's especially odd considering we're still close to the fire lookout tower." This time Lily dismounted in order to examine the remains, which had to be recent. She sifted her cowboy boot through it. Finding nothing, she turned to get on her horse and saw something in the vegetation a few feet away.

"Well, what do you know." Her heart raced. "Two cigarette butts."

"What's so important about that?"

"Porter said the perp had been smoking and they took the butts to the forensic lab to be analyzed. It turned out they were cigarillos. I'm going to take these with me."

Lily reached in her backpack for the empty baggie that had held her sandwich. Using her neck scarf, she picked them up and put them in the baggie before sealing it. "I could be wrong, but I bet that creep is still hanging around here for some reason. I've got to let Porter know!"

After taking pictures with her phone, she put everything in her backpack and they continued to scour the area. Around four they both received a text message that the fallen plane had been spotted in another grid. The search was over.

"Thank heaven it's been found," Lily murmured soberly.

"Amen. Ted will be thrilled I don't have to stay out here overnight. With our wedding in two weeks, we don't have much more time to make all our plans."

"I hear you." But in truth Lily's mind was on Porter, who needed to know what she'd discovered ASAP.

When they reached Glimpse Lake and checked in with Marjorie, Lily loaded her horse in the trailer, said goodbye to Deedee and drove her truck back to town. She headed straight for Porter's ranch. Maybe he wouldn't be there, but she knew this was a vital find.

This was police business. She had a legitimate excuse to approach her patient. That's what she had to keep telling herself.

Porter had just come home from work when his doorbell rang. Tonight he wasn't expecting friends. It was a good thing since he wasn't in the mood to be sociable.

Lily was up in the mountains, where that lunatic

might still be. Knowing she could be in danger, he'd grown restless and wouldn't sleep until she got home safely tomorrow.

He'd decided not to answer it, but whoever it was rang it again. It could be any one of the guys and they wouldn't give up. Letting out a frustrated sigh, he slowly got up from the chair and walked with care through to the living room to answer it.

When he opened the door, he was blown away by the sight of the most beautiful woman he'd ever known adorned in her cowboy hat and Western attire. She'd never come to his ranch before, but seeing her here was a dream come true.

"*Lily!* I thought you were up in the mountains with the brigade."

"I was, but the plane was found. I realize I'm the last person you expected to see, but I've brought you something that couldn't wait." She held what looked like a sandwich baggie in her hand.

"Come in."

"I wouldn't bother you, but this could be important so I'll come in for a minute. Thank you." She moved past him.

He closed the door and invited her to sit down on the couch.

"I will after you do."

Porter smiled and did as she asked with care. "What has brought you here?"

"Today Deedee and I came across two dead campfires near the Crow's Nest, where we were searching for the plane. At the first one I found nothing, but at the second one I found these. More cigarette butts." She handed him the bag. "I used my neck scarf so my fingers wouldn't come in contact with them."

Porter took it from her, so astonished that she'd come, it took a minute to register what she'd brought him. He lifted the bag and examined them.

"Do they look like the cigarillos you told me about last week?"

"Only Cyril will be able to tell, but it's more than possible," he answered. "Which means someone is still up there lighting illegal fires, maybe even the culprit. You're amazing, you know that?"

She blushed but he could tell his praise resonated with her.

"Stay right there while I call Holden." He reached for his cell on the end table. "I need to get on this immediately."

"I'd better get back to the ranch," she said, rising. "Trixie is still out in the trailer."

"Then you go ahead. I'll follow in a few minutes in my car because we need to talk."

"You're not feeling discomfort from driving?" she asked.

"As long as I'm careful, none."

She looked hesitant before nodding. "I'll see you soon then."

He watched her hurry out the door while he got his friend Holden on the phone.

"This could definitely be the break we've been waiting for, Porter. Your therapist is in the wrong line of work."

"Oh, no, she isn't—otherwise we'd never have met."

"If you're saying what I think you're saying, nothing could make me happier." He paused. "By nightfall a trap will be set for whoever it is. In the meantime I'll come by your ranch and collect the evidence."

"I won't be here. I'm driving over to the Owens ranch, but I'll leave the door unlocked and put the baggie on one of the end tables in the living room."

"Perfect."

His adrenaline surged as he made his way outside and got into his car the way Helen had taught him. After starting the engine, he left for her family's ranch. When he drove around back, he found her parked near the barn.

He got out and paced himself as he walked inside. "Lily?"

"Back here."

Porter followed her voice and found her hatless in Trixie's stall, brushing her down. "Have you even had dinner yet?"

"No. I was in too big a hurry to show you what I'd found to stop for anything else."

"Then as soon as you've put your baby to bed, let's go out for a meal to talk. I owe you big-time for a lot of reasons."

Her soft chuckle warmed him. "That sounds good. One bologna sandwich six hours ago didn't quite do the trick." After stuffing the hay net and providing water, she hugged her horse's neck and they left the barn.

She hurried to get in his car. So far his patience had paid off to the point that she was willing to go to dinner with him. Porter was determined that this was only the beginning.

"Because of your quick thinking, Sheriff Granger is already planning to hunt down and bring in the person responsible for that second illegal campfire. With those cigarette butts headed for forensics as we speak, we'll know shortly if the same person is responsible." If the culprit was Melissa's brother... "You may have helped us solve this problem sooner than I would have imagined. I'm indebted to you, Lily."

"Don't give me any credit. I was already up there with Deedee looking for that downed plane." She was modest, too. "Thank goodness it was found."

"Agreed, but I'm talking about the fact that you listened to everything I told you when I first showed up at the clinic. For you to notice those cigarette butts at the other campsite was a brilliant find."

"I couldn't help but remember, not after what happened to you and your poor horse."

He pulled in to The Wok, a local Chinese restaurant, and escorted her to a booth. She sat across from him.

"How's your back?"

"I'm good."

After their order was taken, she pulled out her phone.

"I took some pictures of the campfire and surrounding area. Maybe they won't be helpful." Her presence of mind continued to impress him. She scrolled to the photos and handed it to him.

"Forensics will want to see these. Mind if I forward them to the sheriff right now?"

"Of course not."

After he'd sent them with an accompanying message, their food arrived. Judging by the way her meal disappeared, she really was hungry. She finally sat back. "That hit the spot. Thank you."

It thrilled him to be sitting here with her like this. "If anyone needs to be thanked, it's you. I was worried the minute I knew you'd be searching for the plane up there."

"I phoned our brigade captain and she told everyone to be on the lookout for the fugitive before we started the search. Deedee and I were both armed."

"Armed or not, a desperate fugitive runs on adrenaline that makes him think he's invincible," he warned.

"Well, nothing happened and I won't be going up there again."

"That's the second-best news I've had all day."

A slow smile curved her lips. "What was the first?"

"To discover you on the other side of my front door earlier. I couldn't talk you into coming to my house last week, but now that you have, I'm hoping this was the first of many visits, impromptu or otherwise."

She averted her eyes.

"Surely it hasn't escaped your notice that I'd like to get to know you better, Lily. But if there's a man in your life, then I wish you'd tell me now."

Her head lifted so their gazes met. "There's no one."

Third-best news of the day.

"Then there has to be a gut-wrenching reason why, because I know of at least four men since meeting you at the clinic who would sell their souls to have a shot with you."

He heard her breath catch. "After my crash in Whistler, I learned through a friend that the Olympic racer I'd planned on marrying was married to someone else and had lied to me that he was single. I lay in my hospital bed realizing my future life didn't include marriage or being a skier after all."

Porter groaned. "That explains it."

"If or when I'm ever open to a relationship again, I'll have to have the man investigated by someone I trust, probably my father. He's never lied to me about anything."

Whoa. He sat back to drink his coffee. "I'll tell you whatever you want to know about me right now. But, of course, that assumes you're interested enough to want details."

She cocked her dark head. "You don't mince words, do you?"

"I've taken a page out of your book." But she wasn't ready, and this conversation needed to come to an end. He reached for his wallet and put some bills on the table. "I, too, value honesty above all else. Come on. I'll run you back to the ranch. You must be exhausted after the day you've put in on the mountain."

Within twenty minutes, he turned in to her ranch and drove around back to the rear entrance.

"Don't get out, Porter. You've moved enough for today."

He smiled at her. "Thank you for all you did earlier to help the police find the culprit. I'm thankful that all of you in the brigade returned safely."

"Porter—"

"Yes?" He waited with bated breath.

"Thank you for dinner." That wasn't what she'd been about to say, he mused—he figured she'd changed her mind, but he was pleased by this much progress. "I enjoyed it very much."

"So did I. Good night. I'll see you on Monday at ten."

He sat behind the wheel until she'd let herself in the back door before he took off for his ranch.

Lily spent a wretched Sunday waiting for Monday to come around when she could talk to Porter. Their evening shouldn't have ended the way it had. He'd finally admitted he'd like to spend more time with her, and what did she do? Tell him she would have to have him investigated by her father in order to trust him. She cringed inwardly. What in heaven's name had gotten into her?

Something was seriously wrong with her to be this cynical and jaded. So far Porter had been open with her about everything. It all came down to the fact that she was afraid of falling in love again and getting hurt. That meant she'd given Steve Louter all the power for eight years to close her off to other men, and for what?

Porter didn't deserve any of this. All men were presumed innocent until proven guilty. When had her common sense been so overtaken by such irrational fear that she'd lost her way and her faith in humankind?

Even if she shouldn't be seeing a patient outside hospital hours, it was too late now. She would start all over again with Porter on Monday. Of course, she might have done so much damage already, he was no longer interested in her. The thought of that happening was pure torture.

Lily found herself trembling with nerves on Monday when he was wheeled into her room at ten, ready for another workout.

"Thanks, Ron." She heard him address the orderly before the man left them alone.

"Good morning, Porter." Her heart leaped at the sight of his rock-hard body.

"It *is* a good one." His smile elated her. "On my way over here, I heard from the sheriff. Forensics got back to him. The cigarillo butts and photos you brought to me proved the culprit made that second campfire. Because of you, there's a manhunt up there right now looking for him. If he's caught, you'll be given official credit."

She shook her head. "The only thing I want is that he has to answer to you in a court of law for what happened that night. When I think how he ran away... I can only imagine how you must have felt lying there in the dark with your horse in agony." It embarrassed her how her voice shook, but she couldn't help it.

"Luckily my life was spared. Because of your expertise, I'm walking around almost as good as new, and riding a horse again." As if to prove it, he got out of the wheelchair in his stocking feet and with pure male grace climbed up on the therapy table the way she'd shown him. "I'm ready when you are."

He possessed an incorrigible trait she loved and warmth flowed through her as she walked over to him. "If you'll lie back, we'll begin."

After he'd done her bidding, she put him through the

exercises, taking longer than usual to make sure she was doing a thorough job. "How's the pain?"

"I don't feel any."

Lily had to believe him because she neither saw nor felt any tension lines. She'd tried so hard not to be affected by their nearness, but it was no use. Touching him stirred her senses and it took every ounce of willpower she possessed to remove her hands.

"Are we through?" he asked.

"Yes." She went over to the computer to log in her notes of today's workout. Much as she wanted to talk to him, she would have to wait until this evening because she had another patient coming.

He eased himself carefully off the table and walked over to the wheelchair. "I'll see you tonight at six?"

She nodded. "Dash will be waiting."

"You think he misses me?"

"I wouldn't be surprised," she said, glancing over her shoulder at him as Ron came in to wheel him away.

The rest of the day dragged until she was able to drive back to the ranch. Before Porter arrived, she freshened up, then hurried into the kitchen for something to eat. Her mom was already there shelling peas for their dinner.

"Oh, good. You're home! The roast will be done in a half hour and the three of us can catch up."

"I'd love it another time, Mom." They hugged. "But Porter Ewing is coming in twenty minutes." Her mom knew all about him except for the fact that Lily had fallen for him. She made herself a peanut butter sandwich. "This will have to hold me until later."

"Does Dash seem the right fit for him?"

"He's perfect."

"You mean Dash, or Porter?" her mom teased gently. "I caught a glimpse of him the last time he was here."

"It's no secret that Ranger Ewing is attractive. I admit it."

"Did the evidence you and Deedee came across help at all in finding the culprit?"

"Yes! Those butts were the same as at the other campfire and had been smoked by the same person as before. Porter says the police are scouring up there now."

"That's wonderful you were able to help."

Lily knew her mother was dying to ask more personal questions, but held back, something Lily appreciated. "How was your day?"

"This morning a young married couple came to look at the Trotters and said they'd be back. Early this afternoon a woman showed up wanting to know all about them. She plans to return again soon to ride one. So all in all it's been a very satisfying day."

"Terrific. Porter is hoping to buy Dash, but he has to work it out with his boss."

Her mom started the peas boiling, then looked at her. "I'm so proud of you."

"What do you mean?"

"The way you help people get back on their feet."

She'd finished making her sandwich. "Not without you providing the horses, plus the love. I'm the luckiest girl in the world to have parents like you. Give Dad a hug for me. I'll see you later."

"Enjoy your ride with Ranger Ewing."

Lily nodded, anxious to apologize for some of the things she'd said to him earlier. She put two water bottles in her small backpack with a blanket and ate her sandwich on the way to the barn. Once she'd bridled and saddled the horses, and led them out to the corral, she went back in for the stool.

He might not like using it, but she wouldn't let him mount without it. At some point he'd be able to do it by himself, but she preferred he act on the side of caution.

Chapter 7

Porter had to be the most punctual man she'd ever known. He pulled up in front of the corral at six on the dot under a semicloudy sky. His arrival filled Lily with so much euphoria, she didn't know how to contain it.

When he got out of his car wearing his Stetson and walked with care toward her, she was sure he'd balk at the sight of the stool this time, but no such thing happened. In fact, from the all-encompassing way he was staring at her, she doubted if he'd even noticed it.

"I've been looking forward to our ride since morning. I'd like to go longer this time."

She'd be glad of the extra time so she could talk to him. "As long as you're comfortable, we can keep going."

"By next week I'm hoping to get back out in the field to my regular duties."

"I didn't know that," she said, deadpan, and mounted her horse to wait for him. He got up on the stool and, with his usual care, moved his leg around to sit on his horse and was ready to ride. They headed out of the corral to the pasture at a slow pace. Her father's property reached into the foothills of the Winds.

"We'll ride to that overlook in the distance and see how you feel."

"Let's do it." The excitement in his voice was contagious.

They didn't need conversation for this to seem right and natural. She felt incredibly safe with him. But her guilt over the things she'd said that morning weighed her down.

When she reached the outcropping of rocks, she turned to him. "If you dismount to take a breather, you won't have the stool to help you get back on. It's up to you, but we might have to call for a helicopter if you get a pain that prevents movement."

He grinned. "I'll stay put this time. What's bothering me is you. I know you've got something on your mind, Lily. I can tell by the shadow in your eyes. This is as good a time as any to tell me what's really nagging at you."

She reached in her backpack and pulled out the water bottles. After handing him one, she opened the top of hers and drank to steady her nerves. "I won't lie. I'm attracted to you, Porter. But your arrival in Whitebark last year comes with a huge question mark. Why would a man of your age from New York, with a full-blown career, suddenly uproot himself to come out here?"

He finished half a bottle. "After the man you loved omitted to tell you he was married, I understand how fearful you must be to trust another guy. So I'll tell you what brought me out here. When you hear why, I guess it'll be a case of whether you believe me or not."

"I *want* to," she replied, her voice wobbling.

For the next ten minutes, he filled in Lily on everything he'd told Holden about Ranger Reiver and her false claim against him. "After multiple times when she connived to be alone with me during our duties, she begged me to get in the tent with her and spend the night after we were snowed in. That did it for me.

"I've had my share of girlfriends over the years, but I was never attracted to her. She was a sick woman. Recently I was relieved to hear good news from my old boss, Commissioner Kroger. He handled the official investigation on her with the authorities. She was fired from the forest service and lost her pension.

"If she'd been pregnant, a simple DNA test would have proven me innocent. But it never came to that because she'd lied about seeing a doctor. There *was* no doctor, no pregnancy. Ranger Archuleta testified under oath that she'd harassed me at every opportunity and knew I'd never spent the night in her tent or mine at any time.

"Those were the grounds for permanent dismissal. The fact that she had a history of coming on to other male rangers during her first three years with the forest service put the final nail in the coffin. They testified against her and it meant she lost her pension, too. You just don't do what she did without serious consequences."

He heard her breath catch. "She sounds very unstable."

"That's the word for her."

"How awful for you. Thank heaven your former boss was such a wonderful friend to you and got you out of there."

Porter nodded. "Though I didn't name her specifically, he'd seen my request for a transfer several months before she told him she was pregnant. It backed up everything. Martin found this position for me in Wyoming and set it all up.

"No one ever knew what happened to me. I was gone the next day and fell in love with the Winds. After talking it over with my mother, who lives in Buffalo, New York, with the man she married, I bought the ranch out here from the sale of my childhood home. As you can imagine, I owe Martin my life."

"Your new boss here is thrilled with you," she interjected.

"He won't be if I don't get healthy soon." Porter studied her for a moment. "Do you have any other questions?"

Her eyes clung to his. "None."

"Like I said, you can believe me or not."

"I *do* believe you, Porter." Her voice throbbed. "I'm so sorry for how distrusting I've been."

He hoped she meant it. No other explanation would satisfy him. "I'm not complaining. Your expertise has saved me from hurting my back permanently. A while ago I was lying on my side in the forest wondering if I'd ever be able to ride a horse again, and here I am now on top of Dash and loving it. Because of this horse you've handpicked for me, I'm almost back in business." Staring deep into her eyes, he said gruffly, "I'll always be indebted to you. You're a wonder, Lily."

"I'm not, but thank you," she whispered.

"Why don't we go back from here. I'm ravenous. After we return to the ranch, let's drive somewhere for a bite to eat."

"I'd love it. Let me take your empty water bottle."

As she put both bottles in her backpack, his cell phone rang. He pulled it out of his shirt pocket before looking at her. "This is from the sheriff. I need to take it."

"Of course."

He reined in and clicked on. "Holden?"

"I'll tell you the details later, but the culprit has been caught and is in jail being booked as we speak. How soon can you get down here to interrogate him?"

Porter's gaze traveled over the gorgeous woman he wanted to spend the rest of his life with, but dinner tonight would have to wait. "I'll be there as soon as I can."

After he hung up, he flicked her another glance. "The police have apprehended the culprit thanks to you. I have to get over to the jail immediately and interrogate him."

"Oh, I'm so glad he's been caught!"

"So am I. Will you go to dinner with me tomorrow night?"

"I'd like that."

They rode toward the ranch house in the distance. He felt lighter knowing she knew the truth about his reason for coming to Wyoming. When they reached the corral, she got off Trixie first and hurriedly put the stool down so he could dismount.

No fast movements, Porter.

He lowered himself to the ground without incident and gave Dash a pat before turning to her. It was a struggle not to reach out and kiss her. "I'll be counting the minutes until tomorrow evening." With that comment he left the corral, taking care to walk to his vehicle.

Their talk had changed his whole world. Going through the process of thinking out each move, he got in behind the wheel and drove to the jail parking area, elated how things had progressed with Lily.

After leaving his Stetson in the car, he exited slowly and walked inside. He found Holden in a room next to the interrogation room and sat down with him. "Sorry. I got here as soon as I could."

His friend studied him with curiosity. "Where were you?"

"Out riding with my therapist."

"How long is she going to stay your therapist?"

Porter grinned. "That all depends."

"For what it's worth, I'm cheering you on. You don't look or act like the same guy we visited in the hospital after your accident."

"I'm not," he said in a husky voice. "I'll give you chapter and verse later. Tell me where the perp was found."

"The officers put out a net of officers up near the second campsite. In the middle of the night one of them saw movement. He signaled his partner and they followed him. To their surprise he headed for the Crow's Nest with a rifle. Maybe the culprit thought you had returned to your post. They subdued him quickly and sent for a helicopter."

"Another rifle," Porter murmured.

"That's right. I've decided he's been hanging around watching the forest rangers, either to spy on them for some reason we have yet to figure out, or he was looking for you and wanted to pick you off. We both know the possible reason why."

"Yup."

"He had to know the law has been looking for him, but he was crazy and desperate enough not to care. They've arrested the goon on several charges. He's dangerous and refuses to cooperate." He looked Porter square in the eye. "I'm positive you're the key, otherwise we'd have several dead rangers by now. More and more I'm thinking he's working with Melissa Reiver, who has a vendetta against you."

"I agree." Porter's jaw hardened. He got up from the chair. "I've got an idea. If you're ready to authorize me, I'll go in the interrogation room right now and see if I can worm any information from him."

"You're authorized! Go ahead. I'll watch and listen from the other side of the glass."

Porter nodded and walked to the interrogation room, being careful not to hurry even though his adrenaline was surging.

The unkempt bearded guy sat in his orange jumpsuit, slouched in a chair, handcuffed with his legs shackled. Porter lowered himself down in a chair on the opposite side of the table, always careful to use his legs, not his back, as Lily had taught him.

"I know your name's not Jake, but that's what I'll call you for now." If the culprit was Melissa's brother, he realized that both of them had dark hair, but that still didn't have to mean anything. "It must have galled you when I spotted your little campfire in the middle of the night before you were able to pick me off."

"Go to hell!"

Porter smiled. "You've made a lot of mistakes waiting for me to show up again, especially building another campfire so close to the first one at the scene of the crime."

"What crime?" he bit out.

"Stalking me, for one. But off the top of my head I can think of six, all federal offenses that will put you in prison for a long time. Interesting that you seem to have a real love for Captain Black cigarillos. Such a bad habit," he said, tsking. "That's not a top seller out west, but the New Yorkers love them and it appears you're addicted."

The moment he said it, the guy shot straight up in alarm trying to get out of the chair, but couldn't.

Porter had hit the jugular.

He knew Holden was standing on the other side of the glass separating the rooms and would have noticed the immediate change in their prisoner. Porter's pulse sped up.

"You're in serious trouble, *Jake*. We know you're not operating alone while you aid and abet your sister."

The culprit's dark eyes flashed pure hatred. *Bingo!*

"You can talk now and save us a lot of trouble. Otherwise we'll see you in the morning when you're arraigned before the judge."

An unrepeatable epithet escaped the prisoner's lips.

Porter watched the man squirm, then got up and left the room. Holden was right outside the door, obviously having seen and heard everything. They started walking through the complex to his office in the other part of the building.

Once behind his desk, Holden got on the phone. When he hung up, he said, "Commissioner Kroger is sending me and Stan her picture."

"Don't forget she handles a rifle like a professional."

"I hear you, Porter. The second you hit the jackpot in there, I realized the two of them are working in concert. I'm calling the police chief. He knows what a dangerous situation this is for the rangers. Coupled with your description, we'll put out an APB and arrest her in case she's anywhere around here."

"She and her brother are mental cases, Holden."

"Yup. We don't know how long he's been out here and if his sister came with him, but this means you, Lily Owens and her family are targets. Lily particularly. Melissa is a woman scorned and if she finds out you're involved with anyone, her jealousy will be off the charts."

"That's what I'm afraid of," Porter rasped. He'd never get over it if Melissa hurt Lily.

"I'm ordering 24/7 protection for all of you, effective now. Security will have to be doubled at the clinic while you're still receiving therapy."

"I need to call Lily."

"Let's do that right now on my office phone. I'll put it on speaker. If her parents are there, ask them to listen in and we'll have a conversation with them so they'll understand what's happening."

Porter's body flooded with more adrenaline as he made the call.

Lily was in the kitchen with her parents, ecstatic that the culprit had been caught. While she ate one of her mother's brownies, she told them about her talk with Porter and the experience that had brought him out to the Wind River Mountain Range in the first place.

Her dad looked pensive. "He went through a horrendous ordeal."

"How cruel of that ranger to accuse him like that," her mom groused. "She *is* sick."

"It's awful to think someone could do that to anyone," Lily murmured. "I want you to meet him when he comes for another ride."

Just then her cell phone rang, interrupting her. She checked the caller ID. "It's Porter. He's probably calling from the jail. Excuse me for a minute." She hurried into the dining room for privacy and clicked on, afraid he was phoning to cancel their dinner date.

"Hi, Porter!"

"Lily—"

She blinked. "Your voice sounds odd. Are you all right?"

"I am now that I know *you* are."

Lily gripped her phoned tighter. "What do you mean?"

"Sheriff Granger is on speakerphone with me. Are your parents there?"

"Yes?" She couldn't imagine what was going on.

"He wants to have a five-way conversation."

A chill ran down her body. "All right. They're in the kitchen. I'll go in and put my phone on speaker." She hurried back to the kitchen and looked at her parents. "Porter is with the sheriff. He wants to talk to all of us."

Perplexed, her parents gathered around the phone. "We're listening, Sheriff."

"Mr. and Mrs. Owens? Ms. Owens? This is Sheriff Granger. Ranger Ewing is here in my office with me. We've arrested the culprit that Ranger Ewing tangled with in the mountains recently. Tonight a lot more information has come forth."

Lily started to tremble.

"We have reason to believe he's the brother of Ranger Melissa Reiver."

"Her *brother*?"

"Yes. As he told you, she's a former member of the US Forest Service in New York who was the cause of Ranger Ewing being transferred to Wyoming."

A gasp escaped Lily's lips. "I was just telling my parents about what happened to him."

"Because of her obsession with him, she was fired and stripped of her pension for trying to get her revenge on him. We don't have a name on this brother yet, but it's clear he has been hunting for Ranger Ewing."

Lily couldn't stop shivering.

"It's vital you know the facts. While Ranger Ewing was interrogating him earlier, he learned enough to realize the man's sister is probably out here with him and hiding somewhere nearby. She's a former ranger and is armed and dangerous. It's possible that when she realizes her brother has been arrested, she'll not only attempt to harm Ranger Ewing, but any people he cares about. That makes *you* a target, Ms. Owens."

Hearing that news, Lily found it impossible to swallow.

"I've been in touch with the chief of police and he has sent out officers to your ranch to protect you and your family 24/7 until she's arrested if that's the case. Captain Sanchez will be in charge and will contact you.

"Ms. Owens? We're putting the clinic where you work under twenty-four-hour surveillance since Ranger Ewing will still be going in for more therapy. Our hope is that this will draw Ms. Reiver out of hiding if she's here and we'll be able to make an arrest."

Lily was trembling. "I see."

"There's an APB out on her here and in New York. Ranger Ewing will supply you with a photograph of her when we obtain one so you can be on the watch for her. In the meantime, I'm advising you to take every precaution to protect yourselves."

"Of course. It's a miracle nothing worse has happened yet," Lily responded.

"Amen. I understand your family sells Missouri Fox Trotters and people come to your ranch to buy them. That means everyone, including Ms. Owens's patients who are driven to the ranch for therapy, could be in danger. Keeping all that in mind, if you have any questions, call me at this number and ask for me directly."

Her father cleared his throat. She'd never seen him look so sober. "Thank you for everything you're doing, Sheriff. Be assured my wife and I will do all we can. I'll inform all the ranch hands tonight. We'll pray this woman is caught ASAP if she's here."

"We're going to make sure of it."

Lily heard the click and threw back her head. "I can't believe this woman is after him. It's so horrific, I feel like I'm trapped in a nightmare."

"Let's hope it's over in another day or two." Her dad finished off a cold glass of water. "Assuming she's in Whitebark, we're going to make it damn difficult for her to get to you. Until she's caught, no more visitors to the ranch."

"That one woman might come by," her mother interjected.

Her father shook his head. "If she does, we'll make sure we're all heavily guarded."

Just then Lily's phone rang again.

"It's Porter. Just a minute." She hurried back in the dining room to talk to him alone. "Porter?"

"I know this call had to be shocking to you, but I swear I won't let anything happen to you, Lily. We're going to do everything possible to keep you safe."

"*You're* the one I'm worried about," she cried.

"Holden and I have been talking. You're a target no matter what, so until this is over, I won't be coming out to your ranch or seeing you except at the clinic for my therapy sessions. That will cut down on the chances of her trying to hurt you."

"Do you believe she's in town?" she whispered.

"I do. Don't forget she hates me and I'm the one she's after. Much as I'd love to have dinner with you tomorrow night, there can't be any more dinners until she's arrested."

Pain and regret swept through her.

"She's going to be found soon, Lily."

"I have to believe that." She half groaned the words.

"You'll have full police protection around the clock, but for the next little while, please keep a low profile."

She sucked in her breath. "Of course."

"Can you fit me into your schedule for tomorrow? It's Tuesday, not my usual day, but it's important."

"Of course. I'll ask Matt to take over for me. When will you come?"

"After I've been to her brother's arraignment before the judge, I'll show up at noon with lunch and we'll talk."

At least she'd be able to see Porter tomorrow. Since talking to the sheriff and being warned of the danger, she couldn't imagine her life without him in it.

"Come whenever you can, but please be careful. Promise me you won't let anything happen to you."

"I was just about to tell you the same thing. Good night, Lily."

"Good night."

Still shuddering over the threat that the unstable Ranger posed to all of them, she hung up and walked back to the kitchen.

Her father gave her a hug, but he hadn't finished laying down the law. "Your mom and I have decided you'll have to end all therapy sessions here at the ranch until that woman is caught."

Lily nodded. "Porter already told me as much. He won't be coming to ride, either. The only place I'll be seeing him is at the clinic for his therapy."

Her mom slid an arm around her shoulders. "That's the best plan, honey. It's a miracle that brother of hers didn't kill Porter on the mountain the night of the accident."

"I'm so thankful for that, too," Lily whispered. "Somehow he knew Porter had been assigned to the fire lookout, but didn't expect he would come to investigate his little campfire in the middle of the night. When Porter caught him off guard and confiscated his rifle, he ran off after the accident. It wouldn't surprise me if he hoped Porter wouldn't be found and that he died."

"Let's be grateful he's recovered. I have every faith his sister will be caught now. Sheriff Granger has already set a plan in motion and has a reputation for being a formidable adversary."

"I know."

"But we all have to be vigilant," her father reminded her. "Until this is over, I'll be asking Stuart to take care of your horse. No riding for you. If this woman was a forest ranger, then she was trained to be a marksman who could pick you off from a distance."

"Don't worry, Dad. I won't take any chances and don't want either of you hurt. I'm so sorry that this affects you, too."

Her mom eyed her with concern. "You look exhausted, honey. Why don't you go on up to bed."

"I'm going, but I doubt if any of us will get sleep."

Her dad hugged her again. "If you want company, why don't we all go in the den and watch TV."

She smiled at him. "I love you for saying that, but it's okay. I want to be alone."

Lily needed to cry her eyes out in private. Not only because of fear for Porter's safety, but also because she'd kept him at arm's length since they'd met. Now that he'd told her the truth about himself, she couldn't wait to be with him, but fate had stepped in. The thought of anything happening to him was anathema to her. She ached to be held in his arms, ached to be kissed into oblivion.

Chapter 8

After leaving the arraignment the following morning, Porter picked up some hamburgers and fries and headed for the clinic, aware there were several undercover officers following him. Others had been stationed at the clinic inside and out to protect Lily.

When he arrived in the patient parking area, Ron was waiting with the wheelchair. If Melissa was anywhere around, then she could see that life was going on as usual for him.

Ron wheeled him inside and knocked on the closed door to her room.

"Come in."

Porter breathed a huge sigh of relief to hear Lily's voice.

The orderly pushed him over to her desk, but Porter didn't see Lily at first. He looked around and then noticed her over by a wall cabinet. She glanced at him. "Thanks, Ron."

"Sure. I'll be waiting out in the hall, Mr. Ewing."

"Thank you."

He left the room.

Lily wore another top beneath her lab coat, this one a brilliant shade of blue. The contrast of her lavender eyes and her black hair knocked him over. "How did you sleep?" he asked when he could find his voice.

"I didn't." She walked toward him and sat down at her desk, next to him. "I don't know how you can sleep, either."

"Not well." His eyes drifted over her. "As long as we're being honest, I was holding my breath until I saw you just now."

"I know the feeling." She cleared a spot on her desk. "Thank you for the food. Hand me the sack and I'll put it out for us."

He gave her the food. "I didn't bring drinks."

"We don't need them."

Unable to stand it any longer, he got out of the wheelchair and pulled her to her feet. "What I do need is to kiss you, Lily, or I'm not going to make it another second."

"Neither am I…" But her words were smothered as his mouth descended over hers. It felt like he'd been waiting all his life for the taste and feel of her. He drew her lovely body into his arms until there was no air between them. She smelled divine and melted against him.

Their emotions were full-blown. Nothing was tentative, as one soul-destroying kiss followed another. Her hungry response let him know she'd been wanting this since they'd first met.

"Do you have any idea how beautiful you are? How long I've been waiting for this?" he whispered at last.

Her eyes were glazed as she looked at him. "There were times during your therapy when I came close to forgetting I was your therapist. I was dying for you to kiss me."

"Now she tells me."

Their kisses grew deeper and he forgot where he was until the phone rang on her desk. Even then he didn't want to give her up, but he had to. This was her office for goodness sake, not the place to make love to her the way he wanted. He had to stop, but didn't know how. Holding her in his arms was heaven.

The phone rang a second time. At this point he forced himself to let her go and sat back down in the wheelchair so she could answer it. His body throbbed with desire.

When she picked up, he could hear her voice shaking. For the last few minutes they'd forgotten everything and everyone except how they felt in each other's arms. He'd never experienced passion like this in his life.

The conversation didn't last long. Not looking at him, she sank down in her chair like she was in shock.

"I hope you realize I'm not going to apologize for kissing you, Lily Owens." He was still out of breath.

"Please don't. It's something I've been wanting for a long time, too."

Her honesty was a miracle. "Was that an emergency?"

"No. My next patient just arrived, but Matt isn't here to help, so they'll just have to wait."

"I know you had to fit me in. I'll eat fast." He reached for a burger and some fries.

"What happened at the arraignment, Porter?"

"Her brother pled not guilty. They always do. His trial is set for a month from now. He was charged with lighting fires on federal land without a permit, hunting without a permit, carrying weapons without a permit, leaving the scene of an accident after I'd fined him, giving false information as to his name and employment, trespassing and stalking. Those are just for starters."

She didn't touch her food. Instead, her head lifted and she shot him a stricken glance. "His sister is out there looking for you. I can't bear it." She got to her feet, clinging to the back of her swivel chair. "I'm terrified for you."

"Now you know how I feel, realizing she could be hunting for you, too. We'll both have to be extra careful until she's arrested."

"But what if she isn't?" she cried.

"She will be. Holden always gets the culprit. I want your promise you'll go home straight after work and stay there. I'll be calling you every so often to know you're all right."

Lily nodded. "Promise me you won't let anything happen to you."

"Nothing's going to happen to either of us. Now I have to go."

"Not yet." Her eyes pled with him to stay.

"Your patient is waiting and I've got to get to head-quarters." Remembering her Wednesday schedule, he said, "I'll see you tomorrow afternoon at three."

"I don't know if I can wait that long."

"You took the words out of my mouth." Before he did something like pull her into his arms again and never let her go, he wheeled around and headed for the door.

"Porter?"

When he looked over his shoulder, he saw her hurry across the room. She threw her arms around his neck and kissed the side of his head. The touch of her lips shot through to his insides. "Please stay safe."

"That goes for you, too." He turned and kissed her mouth long and hard before letting her go. "I'll call you later."

She opened the door for him. Her eyes clung to his until Ron rolled him down the hallway out of her sight. "You weren't in there very long."

"Nope."

Ron had no clue how much pain Porter was in because he'd had to leave her. This was agony on a level he couldn't imagine. Once they went out the clinic doors, Porter told him to stop.

"I can make it from here, Ron."

"No, you can't, or I'll get fired." He wheeled him to Porter's car in the parking lot.

"Thank you." Gingerly, he got out of the wheelchair and climbed into the car. Out of the corner of his eye, he saw one of the unmarked cars following him as he left to meet Holden. The only way he could handle this was knowing that Lily was being protected.

Ten minutes later Stan joined them at the sheriff's office to discuss the situation. By now Martin Kroger had sent the photo of Melissa from his files and her picture had been disseminated to all law enforcement in Sublette County. Every officer and forest ranger needed to be on constant alert. No one was safe.

Porter knew there was a volatile side to Melissa. When she found out her brother had been arrested, she would be enraged. Perhaps she already did know and was out hunting for him. Nothing would stop her from trying to kill him. His only hope was that she didn't know about Lily yet.

At five, Lily said goodbye to her last patient and left the clinic for home. Though she knew she was being guarded, the idea that a lunatic woman was out there somewhere with a weapon chilled her to the bone. She didn't stop for anything on the way to the ranch.

Once she'd driven around the back, she hurried inside and locked the door before calling to her parents. When she didn't get an answer, she phoned her mom and learned they were out in the barn, showing their horses to a possible buyer who'd come before. They'd be in a little later and were thrilled she was home safe.

Lily went upstairs to shower and change, her whole mind and heart on Porter. She could still remember what he'd told her about the ranger. *She begged me to get in the pup tent with her and spend the night. I was suspicious.*

By rejecting her, the woman had lost her mind enough to talk her brother into helping her find Porter no matter how long it took. After a year of looking for him, who knew what plan she had in store for him? Entrapment? Torture? A slow death? Did she know by now her brother had been arrested?

Shudder after shudder racked Lily's body. When her phone rang, she saw that it was her mother and picked up. "Mom?"

"Hi, honey. Now that those people have gone, come on downstairs. We'll all cook dinner together."

"I'm going to be terrible company."

"Couldn't Porter keep his appointment today?"

Her breath caught in remembrance of what had gone on in the therapy room. "H-he came right on time," she stammered. But Lily wouldn't be seeing him again until three tomorrow and didn't know how she would bear it. She hadn't been the same since.

"Any new developments?"

"Not yet," she replied.

"I see. What are you doing right now?"

Lily swallowed hard. "If you want to know the truth, thinking horrible thoughts."

"Join the club." Her mother's unfailing sense of humor was the tonic she needed.

"I'll be down in a minute."

"I've already started counting. We're going to make it through this, honey."

Before she went to bed later, Porter phoned and said virtually the same thing. "I'm certain Melissa knows her brother has been arrested. They had to have been staying somewhere in town and she now realizes he's been caught. In her desperation she'll make her move soon. Just stay indoors until you have to go to work. This will be over before we know it. I'm living for tomorrow, when I see you at three."

Her eyes closed tightly. "I can't wait."

"Neither can I."

After they hung up, she turned on the television and watched reruns of some old TV sitcoms. She had no idea when she fell asleep, but awakened late Wednesday morning, which didn't matter since she wouldn't be going anywhere until afternoon.

Trying to fill her time, she showered and washed her hair, wanting to look beautiful for Porter. After going downstairs she fixed breakfast and phoned Millie to find out how she was doing. Lily didn't tell her what was going on so it wouldn't upset her.

There was another call for the brigade to look for an autistic boy who'd wandered from his parents' camp in the mountains. Normally Lily would have asked for the day off to help in the search, but not this time. Porter didn't want her leaving the ranch until she drove into work.

When two thirty crept around, she left for the clinic, unable to stand the inactivity any longer. She wouldn't be able to breathe until she saw Porter.

"Lily? Can I have a word with you?"

Matt was coming out of his office. "Yes, but I'm expecting my next patient in five minutes."

"All I wanted was to remind you of the hospital board

dinner coming up this Saturday evening at the White-bark Hotel. You and I have been invited to attend."

"That's right. I forgot. Thank you for telling me."

"I'd be happy to come by for you."

She couldn't believe he'd just said that, not after she'd made herself clear. "I'll get there on my own, Matt, but I appreciate the heads-up."

"It's been on the calendar for a month. The director wants to know if you're coming."

"I'll contact him right away." Since meeting Porter, everything else had gone out of her mind. "Thanks, Matt."

Lily walked on down the hall to the closet for a clean lab coat. After putting it on, she hurried to the therapy room. But she was so filled with anxiety that Porter might not show up, she'd turned into a nervous wreck.

No sooner had she approached her desk than there was Ron's knock on the door.

Her heart leaped. "Come in."

She turned around as the orderly opened it. Porter got out of the wheelchair, thanked Ron and entered the room, shutting the door behind him. Today he wore his forest-ranger uniform. Dressed in official gear and boots with the badge on his pocket, the works, he looked transformed and imposing. His male potency was so striking, her legs felt like mush.

"That's a far cry from your hospital jammies, Mr. Ewing. Is this some kind of statement?"

He locked the door. That gesture alone set her pulse racing. "Today I woke up feeling my old self, thanks to you. I couldn't get here soon enough."

The fire in his eyes propelled her toward him. They met halfway and he pulled her into his arms, crushing her against him. Burying his face in her hair, he said, "If I hadn't heard your voice just now, I'm not sure what I would have done."

In the next breath, his mouth covered her own. For him to be here in her arms was all she wanted out of life as they attempted to assuage their insatiable longing for each other.

Before she knew what was happening, he pulled her to her swivel chair, then sat down next to her. "I'd lower us to the mat on the floor, but if I did that, I'd never let you up again."

"Oh, Porter—"

After giving her another long, deep kiss, he raised his head. "I didn't come here today for another therapy session. I came to make sure you're all right. As soon as this case is solved, I'll make the arrangements to buy Dash," he whispered against her lips. "We'll go for a campout in the mountains, where we can be completely alone. I need time with you."

"We both need it," she said, giving him a kiss that went on and on, filling her with an ecstasy she'd never dreamed of. When her desk phone rang she ignored it until she heard Cindy's voice.

"Lily? Ron came by for your patient, but I guess you didn't hear him knock. Your next appointment is here."

She let out a groan of protest, not wanting to let Porter go, but she had to. Easing herself away from him with reluctance, she turned to her desk. "I need five more minutes with my patient, then send Ron. After you see Ranger Ewing leave, you can tell my next patient to come in."

"Will do."

Porter's arms crept around her waist and he kissed the back of her neck. "Every part of you is so tempting, I can't leave you alone."

She whirled around in his arms. "I don't want you to leave. Every time we have to say goodbye, I'm afraid."

"We're going to get through this, Lily." He stole another kiss, then reached in his pocket and pulled out a folded paper. "This is the photo of Melissa sent from New York. Take it to show your folks. Now I'd better get out of here, or we're going to cause a traffic jam in the clinic that'll bring the media to find out why." He glanced around. "I see you've got a surveillance camera in the corner."

"True, but it didn't catch us."

"If it did, I want it."

She broke into gentle laughter. "I need to do a lot of things, like apply fresh lipstick and brush my hair."

His slow smile turned her heart over. "You look thoroughly ravished... I love that look on you."

Lily gripped his hard-muscled upper arms. "I hope you haven't hurt your back holding me."

"I'm fine."

"Please, please, don't let anything happen to you, Porter."

He brushed his lips against hers. "Now you know how *I* feel every second I'm away from you. I'll phone you tonight. If you need anything, call me."

"I promise."

They kept kissing each other until Ron's tap sounded against the door. She unlocked it, then hid behind it as Porter walked out. Before her next patient arrived, she hurried to her desk for her purse to repair the damage.

The day droned on before she could leave the clinic at seven. Before she left, she studied the copy of the photograph Porter had given her. Melissa Reiver was a good-looking woman. She put it back in her pocket.

It helped to know undercover officers were following her. When she reached the ranch and hurried inside, her parents were in the kitchen cooking dinner.

"Thank goodness you're home safe and sound!" her mother said.

"Hey, Mom," she said, walking over to give her a quick hug. "I've got something to show you and Dad. Porter left it when he came in for his appointment this afternoon." On the way home, the picture of the emotionally disturbed ranger had burned a hole in her jeans' pocket. Now she took it out and spread it on the kitchen counter for her parents to see.

Her mother glanced at it first, then gasped. "Oh, no—come and look," she said to Lily's father. "This is the face of the woman who came to see one of the horses again today!"

"But she had short red hair."

"Yet can't you see that's her face?" her mother asked.

"You're right."

"*Mom*—she was here?" Adrenaline spurted through her veins. "How long ago?"

"About four thirty."

Her father pulled out his cell phone. "I'm calling the sheriff."

Lily's hand trembled as she reached for her own phone to call Porter. He picked up on the second ring.

"Lily? Are you all right?"

"I'm home with my parents, but there's been a development. They took one look at the photograph I brought home and said Melissa had been here at the ranch around four thirty today. But she had short red hair."

"I *knew* it." The way he said it sent shivers down her spine. "Have they called Holden?"

"Dad's on the phone with him right now."

"Good. Stay inside together. I'll be in touch soon." He clicked off before she could say goodbye.

In a minute her father hung up and rejoined them at the kitchen table. "We're to stay put and carry out our normal chores tomorrow," he told her mom. "They're setting up a sting operation, but the sheriff said it might take several days before she's caught."

When he turned his gaze to Lily, the look of calm reassurance in his eyes did little to soothe her frazzled nerves "And Lily? You're to go into work tomorrow as usual. He'll be coordinating everything with Captain Sanchez, who will keep in touch with all of us as things proceed."

While Lily made a green salad to keep from falling apart, Porter phoned her. She left what she was doing and hurried into the dining room.

"Porter?"

"Hey, sweetheart. How are you doing?"

"I've been better," she admitted. "My dad just talked to Holden. The sheriff told him that I should go to work tomorrow."

"It's important you keep sticking to your routine. The fact that Melissa's come to your ranch twice proves she doesn't think you know she's in Whitebark. I'm aware you're frightened, but remember you'll be protected all the way to work and back.

"Stay at the hospital and eat in the cafeteria tomorrow. When you head home, don't go anywhere else. It's vital you stay with your schedule. Holden will be giving you explicit instructions once you're home from the clinic. I'll be working with the officers. This is going to end soon."

"Porter? I couldn't imagine life without you now."

"Don't you know I feel the same way? But this nightmare is close to being over. Remember that."

Porter walked into Holden's office early Thursday morning. Their eyes met as streams of unspoken words passed between them.

"I've got more news this morning, Porter. After feeding the prints on the suspect into the criminal database using the Reiver name, we came up with a suspect operating in New York. He has a string of robberies and aliases. There's a warrant out for his arrest. I've already alerted law enforcement in New York that we've arrested him under the name of Jake Harrison and have sent them all the pertinent information."

"Good grief," Porter murmured. "He and Melissa are both deranged."

"He's twenty-five and was born Jedediah Marsh Reiver in Potsdam, New York. Parents are dead. One sister still living."

"Martin Kroger mentioned that Melissa came from Potsdam originally," Porter mused. "It all fits."

Holden nodded. "He goes by everything from Jed to Jack. It's not surprising he came up with the name Jake."

"His addiction to Captain Black cigarillos proved to be his downfall."

"Yes indeed. And Lily's find in the mountains helped cross all the *t*'s."

Porter took a quick breath just thinking about her. "Yesterday when I called her, she told me her mother recognized the suspect from the photo I've given her, even though Melissa had red hair. Maybe it was dyed, or she was wearing a short red wig. I thought about that all night. It's possible she has a number of different wigs in order to disguise herself. Let's look at the surveillance tape viewing every visitor who has come to the jail since her brother was arrested. If we could study it and spot her, then—"

"Then we'd know those two have communicated," Holden interrupted. "It would give us a timetable for her activities."

"Exactly. Maybe we'll find out she has more than one disguise."

"I've already got it on the screen."

Porter should have known his friend was always ten steps ahead of everyone else. Holden adjusted the monitor so they could both look. "I had the online register of visitors run off for me showing the dates and times of each inmate visit."

"Good." Together they poured over each picture. When a blonde in a medium-length bob appeared at the desk to talk to the deputy in charge of visitors, they both looked at each other.

"Blow it up, Holden."

The second the picture was enlarged on the screen, Porter got to his feet. "That's Melissa! What's the date and time?"

"Yesterday."

Porter turned to the visitor log. "Here it is. Eileen Davies, two twenty p.m." He grimaced. "This means her brother has told her everything and she's known my steps including my visits to the Owens ranch. She's had plenty of time to figure out my therapy schedule and plan her next move. No doubt she intends to kill me and Lily at the same time, while we're out riding away from the ranch house. I need copies of her in red hair, blond hair and her natural brunette hair."

"I'll put Walt Emerson on it right now." Holden picked up the phone to call the under sheriff. After Holden got off the phone he said, "Walt will have those photos for you when you leave my office.

"In the meantime I'll have Captain Sanchez circulate a copy of all three pictures to every hotel, motel, car rental and taxi service around. We may turn up something significant before the day is out."

"Sure hope so." Scrubbing a hand over his jaw, Porter added, "While you're at it, Holden, put the alias she's using into the criminal database with her fingerprints sent from Martin. Who knows what might come up."

"You're reading my mind."

"I'm headed over to the hospital now to show her photos to those people on duty. Someone had to have seen her, or even spotted a car she was driving, unless she walked there or took a taxi."

"Anything's possible. Let's connect later."

"Thanks, man. You'll never know what your help means to me."

"I know," he said quietly. "When Jessica was being targeted, I never slept."

That was the truth.

Porter left Holden's office for Walt's. The under sheriff handed him an envelope with the photos in question and he left for the parking lot. He wanted to run, but knew it was too soon.

For all he knew, Melissa was out there in a car stalking him in plain sight. How ironic when there were surveillance officers protecting him.

On his way to the hospital he had an idea to talk to Ron first. The orderly had an eye out for beautiful women. Every time he wheeled Porter in and out of the hospital, he had a chance to look around, and would notice someone like Melissa. If Porter showed him a picture of her, no doubt Ron would remember seeing her. It was worth a try.

Once he arrived at the hospital, he went up to the surgical ward to talk to the staff and pass around the pictures. No one recalled seeing a woman who fit her description.

He caught up with Ron in front of the elevator.

"Hey, Mr. Ewing. I didn't know you had an appointment."

"I didn't. I'm here on police business. I want to show you something." He pulled the photos out of the envelope. "I need to know if you've seen this woman since I was first brought to the hospital."

Ron studied each one and tapped the one with the blond wig. "I saw her when you got out of the wheelchair yesterday to get in your car."

His pulse quickened. "Was she in a taxi or car?"

"She was parked in one of the handicapped spaces driving an older white Honda."

"Could you tell if it was a rental?"

"I didn't think to look," Ron admitted.

Why would he? "What made you notice her?"

"She was a babe."

"Thanks. You've been more help than you know. If you see her again, call the sheriff's office. Ask for Under Sheriff Emerson and give him any information you can."

"Are you saying she's—"

"She's wanted by the police," he interrupted. "Not a woman you want to know, let alone talk to."

On that note Porter took off for his car, no longer needing to interview anyone else. En route to Holden's office, he phoned Walt to tip him off about the white Honda. Melissa had either been driving a car she'd purchased or rented.

Ten minutes later he reentered Holden's office and

told him what he'd discovered from Ron. "Anything on Eileen Davies?"

His friend shook his head. "But now that the orderly at the hospital has identified her, we know she's ready to make her move. I've been coordinating with the police chief and Captain Sanchez. Everyone's primed to close in. We've already talked to Lily and her parents. Unless you have reservations about this, it's time to put our plan into action."

He clenched his jaw. "I'm more than ready to get this over with and will head over to the Owens ranch right now."

"Lily will have your horse ready to ride and take you into the foothills, where I understand you rode last time. Melissa will have staked out the area ahead of time, but so have we." He got out of his chair and walked around his desk. "I don't have to tell you to watch your back."

He nodded before leaving the complex. Today could be the day this nightmarish situation came to a head. Lily had more courage than anyone he knew, but they were facing an unhinged woman who had no conscience at this point. He phoned Lily as he drove to her ranch to let her know he was on the way.

"Lily? No one is ready for what we're about to go through. But I want you to know you don't have to do this. I'll ride alone and hope this draws her out."

"No…absolutely not. I won't let you go without me!" she cried. "How soon are you coming?"

"I'm close to your ranch now. You sure about this?"

"Yes." She sighed. "Thank goodness you're almost here. Waiting for you is killing me. When I talked to the sheriff, he told me to go through the motions for your therapy like we always do and not deviate. That way we'll hope Melissa isn't tipped off that anything different is going on. I've packed food and drinks in the saddlebag for meals while we're gone and brought an extra blanket."

"That sounds perfect."

"I'll be out in the corral with the horses," she told him.

"How are your parents feeling about this?"

"They want this over, too, and believe we're doing the right thing by drawing her out. As long as I'm with you, I'm not afraid."

He swallowed hard. "During our ride I have more information to tell you." He turned onto the street running past her ranch in the distance. "I'll be there in a few minutes."

"Hurry!"

He said a prayer the rest of the way.

Chapter 9

Lily shook with excitement as she saw Porter pull up near the corral dressed for work. He looked so handsome, she moaned in reaction.

His eyes zeroed in on her mouth and the next thing she knew he was gripping her arms to kiss her, igniting every sensitive nerve in her body. "I needed that," he murmured after lifting his head.

"You think I didn't?" Still wrapped up in his embrace, she gazed up at the overcast sky. The clouds were growing darker. She had a feeling it would rain soon.

"Come on. I'll help you get up on Trixie, but I need another kiss first."

Five minutes later she was breathless before getting on her horse. She watched him use the stool and mount Dash with ultimate male grace. He made a clicking sound and his horse started toward the opening of the corral alongside hers. Once they were out in the pasture and had headed toward the foothills, he angled his head at her.

"There's a lot I need to tell you. This morning Holden and I went through the surveillance tape outside the jail. Melissa showed up to visit her brother, in a blond wig no less."

Lily shook her head. "I guess I shouldn't be surprised."

"Walt Emerson made up some photos for me to show the hospital staff." He told her what he'd discovered at the hospital.

"Trust Ron."

"Yup." He smiled. "Holden's running down every lead, hoping to find out where Melissa has been staying."

A cry escaped Lily's lips. "She's known everything that's been happening around here, hasn't she?"

"I'm afraid so. She was registered on the jail visitor log as Eileen Davies. Holden ran her name and fingerprints through the criminal database, but nothing had shown up when I left his office. Knowing how fast and thorough he is, it won't be long until he's learned everything about her."

As they rode, the wind started up. Lily looked at the sky. "We're in for a storm later."

"Let's ride faster to that outcropping of boulders and eat our lunch."

"We mustn't gallop yet, Porter."

"You're right."

They walked their horses instead. Lily was so thrilled to be with him, she almost forgot they could be in the crosshairs of Melissa's rifle scope. The joy of being with him like this lit up her world.

When they reached the spot, he dismounted first.

"Oh, no—" she protested. "What about your back?"

He walked over to help her down. "I didn't feel even a slight twinge of pain. Come here." Porter reached for her and pulled her into his arms. They clung to each other, overcome with emotions they were unable to suppress. He kissed her with a fierce hunger that opened the floodgates of her desire.

"Lily?" he whispered, sounding out of breath. "I have to tell you now I don't want to live without you. I'm painfully in love with you. Just so you know, I've never said that to another woman in my life."

"I'm in love with you, too," she cried, kissing him desperately. "You've turned my whole world around in ways you can't comprehend. This threat has made me realize how precious life is. I need and want you in my life, even if we haven't known each other that long."

He covered her face with kisses. "I knew how I felt by the end of my first session with you. My desire for you knows no bounds, Lily. When Melissa has been apprehended, you and I have to talk about our future."

Delirious with joy, she gave him another kiss before spreading the blanket on the lush grass. After she sat down, she looked up at him. "Why don't you join me? We're not in the clinic now."

"Lily—"

"This is the one place we can be together without the

hospital knowing about it." She lay back, eyeing him with longing, waiting for him to come to her. "Just remember how to get down so you don't do something that undoes all the progress you've made."

He started toward her with a blazing look in those dark eyes that set her on fire. Lowering himself the way she'd taught him, he shifted to his side and began devouring every inch of her face and neck. Lily was breathless by the time their mouths fused, wanting to show him all the things she felt.

Porter pulled her halfway on top of him while his hands roved over her arms and back. He took her to a different realm, where she forgot everything except to love and be loved.

"I love you so much, Porter. After Steve, I didn't think it was possible to fall in love again. But the moment you and I met, I felt that ice melt from around my heart, yet a part of me was afraid to trust what I was feeling. Keep holding me and never let me go."

"I plan to do that for the rest of our lives, but there's going to be a downpour pretty soon. If you want to eat, we'd better do it now."

"You're right."

He lowered her saddlebag to the blanket, where they could eat behind the tallest boulder. They sat next to each other, enjoying the lunch she'd prepared, but once it was over they couldn't stay out of each other's arms.

"I know we have to head back, but I need this more than my next breath," he rasped, pulling her down next to him. For a little while they gave one kiss after another until she was enraptured and lost count. The world fell away as they sought to bring each other pleasure.

"Do you think she can see us now?" she whispered into his neck.

"I think the boulders are hiding us for the moment. But once we're back on the horses, we're a target."

"Maybe she isn't out here today."

"If not, we'll ride out here again tomorrow until she makes herself known," he told her.

Another gust of wind brought cooler air and the smell of rain. Lily shivered.

"Come on, sweetheart. Let's head back before we're caught in the deluge."

They both stood and packed everything in the saddlebag. He placed it over the back of her horse with care. She followed with the blanket he folded behind her saddle.

"Up you go."

"What about you?" she said in a concerned voice. "You don't have a stool."

"I guess I'm going to find out what it's like to do this the old-fashioned way." After kissing her mouth, he reached for the reins and climbed on Dash, expecting he might experience pain, but all he felt was strain. "So far, so good. That's because you've taken such good care of me."

"Thank heaven you're not in pain."

He grinned over at her. "Are you ready to beat the rain?"

"Yes."

"Let's go."

* * *

They started to walk their horses back and had only gone a couple of hundred yards when a rifle shot zinged past them. "Porter!"

"She's spotted us. Keep going and ride low, sweetheart."

Another fifty yards and another rifle shot filled the air, so close to his ear it caused it to ring. Where in the hell were the deputies? Surely by now they knew her location. There was no shelter out here. The only thing to do was head straight for the ranch.

"Keep your head down, Lily!"

"What about you?" But the second the words came out, they heard a third shot, then another. Lily dropped to the sagebrush with her horse.

Porter's heart came close to failing him. If the fall hurt her spine… The crash that had ended her skiing career eight years ago had already done a considerable amount of damage to her.

He reined in his horse and jumped off to help Lily off her horse. He covered her carefully with his body, but it was like déjà vu to hear her mare screaming in pain. To make things worse, the rain had started in earnest.

"My poor horse—"

"I know. We'll get her help. Lie as still as you can."

"*I've* been hit, too," Lily gasped.

Dear God. He couldn't believe this had happened. "Where are you hurt, darling?"

"My lower left leg."

Hell and Hell. "What about your spine? Do you think

the fall injured you again?" Please, God, don't let this have done more damage. Porter couldn't bear it.

"No. Trixie cushioned my fall completely."

Porter didn't believe her. He phoned Holden, who told him the deputies had caught up to Melissa and she'd been hauled away. But it hadn't happened soon enough for Lily.

"Send a helicopter quick. Lily's been shot in the lower leg. Her horse was hit, too." Trixie was making squealing sounds. Porter was still worried about her spine. Right now she wouldn't be able to know what she was feeling.

He heard a muttered curse come out of his friend. "Help is on the way. Hang in there."

Porter moved so he could inspect her leg. He needed to stop the bleeding. After removing his shirt, he put the badge in his pocket, then bunched it up and pressed it against the wound.

"A helicopter is coming to take you to the hospital. I just talked to Holden. Melissa has been caught and taken away so you don't have to fear her anymore."

"Oh, thank God!" she cried.

"The nightmare is over, sweetheart."

"What about Trixie?"

Her horse was still in terrible pain, but she wasn't screaming as loudly as before. "She was hit in the left back leg, too, but I know you'll both be all right. Just lie still."

In another minute he heard the rotors of two helicopters overhead. When they landed, the area was swarmed by deputies and the paramedics, who gave Lily first aid and lifted her into the medical helicopter.

"Be careful with her in case she hurt her spine," Porter told them. "She had a former injury eight years ago."

"Will do."

He climbed in behind her.

"Get help for that horse, and make sure mine is returned to the ranch safely," he instructed from the doorway.

"Yes, sir."

Soon the helicopter sped through the rain toward the hospital in Whitebark. Porter planted himself on the bench at her side while the paramedics put in an IV with some pain medication and cut the material away from her wound.

"The bullet's right there."

Porter watched as he removed it and bandaged her leg. "Do you think it hit the bone?"

"No. I believe this is a flesh wound that grazed the outside. She's very lucky, but once we're at the hospital they'll x-ray her to be certain she's all right. You did a good job of stopping the bleeding, but I'm afraid your shirt is ruined. When we reach the hospital, they'll give you a T-shirt to put on."

"I'm not worried."

"Porter?"

He looked down at her gorgeous pale face. "Right here, sweetheart. How are you feeling?"

"I'm so thankful she didn't shoot you."

Her love and sacrifice humbled him. "What she did

to you was unforgiveable. Is your back hurting where you had your former injury?"

"Not at all. Nothing matters now because she can't hurt anyone else."

"Not ever," he promised.

"Don't leave me."

He bent down, brushing his lips tenderly against hers. "Where would I go without you? You're my whole life. I'm afraid you're stuck with me forever."

"I adore you. What about Dash?"

"One of the deputies will ride him back to the ranch."

"Can you find out about Trixie? She needs me."

"We all need you, me most of all, but don't worry. We'll know everything by the time we get you to the hospital. Let the medicine help you relax."

"What about my parents?" she asked.

"Holden will have notified them and told them everything. I'm sure they'll be at the hospital soon after we get there."

"I'm going to need therapy for my leg." Her voice sounded sleepy.

"Well, I can tell you right now that Dr. Jensen isn't going to be the one to help you. If you'll teach me what to do, *I'll* be the one to get you back to normal."

"I'd love that…" She was fading fast.

The rain was still coming down hard as the helicopter landed at the hospital. A team of medical staff greeted them and rolled Lily on a gurney into a cubicle in the ER. He told them to have her back checked out as well for any injury she might not be feeling at the moment.

They nodded and he followed them inside, but he was told to wait outside the curtain until they'd checked her out.

Another staff member saw his shirtless condition and found a white T-shirt for him. As he was shrugging into it, a crowd of deputies surrounding the police chief came into the ER, followed by Holden, who made a beeline to Porter.

Their gazes connected before he hugged him. "Thank God you and Lily are still alive."

"Amen to that. You and I both know how much worse it could have been. Do Lily's parents know yet? She was asking about them in the helicopter."

"They're on their way here."

He clenched his jaw. "Tell me what happened out there, Holden."

"Melissa drove into the foothills on a fire break road and camouflaged her car in the shrubbery. Then she very cleverly concealed herself in such a dense copse of trees, it took time for the two deputies nearest her to work their way in to even see her. They exchanged fire with her before she died."

She was dead? "Are the officers all right?"

"Yes."

"I want to thank them personally," Porter said hoarsely.

"You'll get your chance."

"What about her horse?"

"It's already at the vet hospital. The deputies felt her mare was in pretty good shape," Holden answered. "I'll be notified of her prognosis soon."

"Good."

He released a ragged breath. So Melissa was gone… Heaven help Porter, but he wasn't sorry. "She was beyond ill."

"Just like her brother."

Porter eyed his friend. "It's over now. I have to pray Lily's going to recover from this without any serious complications." *Please don't let her spine be hurt again.* "When I think of the crash she suffered in the Olympics and the months of recovery, it's so unfair to think she's been injured again. I shouldn't have let her be a target."

"We've been over this before, Porter. Melissa was waiting to get both of you at the same time."

"But for this to have happened to Lily after all she's done for me…"

Holden gazed at Porter, a look of understanding in his eyes. "Now it's your turn to take care of her. Right?"

He nodded. "You better know it is! But a miracle happened that Lily is still alive."

"And you," Holden reminded him.

"I'll love her forever." Then he nodded at his friend. "Without your help and friendship, this might never have ended the way it did. I owe you."

One of the staff came out of the cubicle. "Mr. Ewing? The doctor says you can come in now. The patient is asking for you."

Holden patted him on the shoulder. "Go on in to her. I'll watch for her parents."

"I'm getting more and more in your debt," he said before hurrying to Lily's bedside.

"Porter—" She was groggy, but awake. "I thought you'd never come."

"That's my fault," Dr. Andrews said. "We had to stabilize you first."

Porter reached for her free hand since the other arm had an IV. "How are you feeling right now, sweetheart?"

"Thankful to be alive and with you."

The doctor smiled at him. "She's a brave woman. I'm happy to tell you the bullet only grazed that part of her leg. You did an excellent job of stopping the bleeding. With bed rest and bandaging, along with antibiotics, she'll be back to normal before long with only a scar to show for it."

"I can live with a scar." Lily's lavender eyes were totally focused on Porter.

Emotion overwhelmed him. "We'll call it your mark of bravery, because that's what you are. The bravest woman I've ever known." He turned to the doctor. "She survived a near fatal crash in the Super G at the Olympics eight years ago and was hospitalized for months."

The other man glanced at Lily in surprise. "You were an Olympian?"

"You didn't need to tell him that, Porter."

"I love to tell everyone how outstanding you are. You would have medaled if the accident hadn't happened. Today you escaped another accident with your life! I think you've been through enough and I couldn't bear it if you've suffered another spinal injury."

The doctor shook his head. "She checks out fine that way, but we'll take an X-ray later if she complains of pain she's not feeling right now. We're moving Ms.

Owens to a private room within the hour. In a few days I'll release her. What she needs right now is rest and care. I imagine you'll help see to that."

"You can count on it."

Porter heard voices on the other side of the curtain. "I think your parents are here."

Dr. Andews pulled aside the curtain and Lily's mother rushed in to kiss her daughter. Her father wasn't far behind. Porter stood back and waited while they hugged and commiserated together while asking the doctor questions.

After he left, Mr. Owens turned to Porter. There was telltale moisture in his eyes. "Thanks for staunching the blood and getting her here so fast. Once again my daughter has escaped tragedy."

"I was just telling the doctor about her accident during the Olympics and said virtually the same thing. But I don't want her to have to go through any more trauma like this again in her lifetime."

"Agreed," he said in a gravelly voice. "We're thankful you're all right and escaped harm, Mr. Ewing."

"Call me Porter."

"Considering how my daughter feels about you, we've already thought of you as Porter for quite a while."

"Considering how she feels about her father, I'll take that as a compliment. She once told me the only man she could ever trust was you."

He chuckled. "I think I don't hold that distinction any longer."

Now it was Porter's turn to smile. "She's my life, sir."

Her father's blue eyes lit up. "Call me Ross."

A warm feeling of belonging swept through Porter as another staff member entered the cubicle and announced they were taking Lily to the third floor. He turned to her and covered her hand.

"Did you hear that, Lily? They're taking you up to my old stomping grounds."

A faint smile broke out on her lips. "It feels like the hospital has become our home."

His throat swelled. "For now." He leaned over to kiss her mouth briefly. "While your parents go with you, I have some things to take care of and will see you in a little while."

For one thing he needed to call his mother and tell her all that had happened before she saw it on the news. This was a big story that would resonate in New York as well as here.

When he stood up, her mother gave him a huge hug. "I'm Caroline. We'll talk later," she whispered. "Bless you for bringing her back home to us."

He cleared his throat. "It took everyone's help including that from above. Tell Lily I'll check in with her a little later."

"Of course."

The second he stepped out of the cubicle he ran into Wyatt.

"You're a sight for sore eyes, Porter. Cole and I cheered to learn that you and Lily were going to be all right once her leg has healed."

"Thanks, Wyatt. The doctor has told me she *will* be fine in time."

"The cheers from the deputies have kept coming to hear that lunatic was taken down for good," his buddy told him. "You two have been through hell."

"You can say that again. I have to tell you I'm glad you're here. Could you run me to the Owens ranch? I left my car there. On the way I'll give you a play-by-play of how everything went down."

"I'm all ears. Let's go, but we'll dodge the reporters and leave the hospital through the exit at the other end of the hall. My car's around the other side of the building." Glancing over at him, Wyatt grinned. "By the way, that's an interesting shirt you're wearing. I didn't know you had one like that in your wardrobe."

A chuckle escaped his lips. "After Lily was shot, I had to use my uniform to stop the bleeding. Someone here in the ER handed me this."

"You look good, dude."

The rain had turned to drizzle by the time they reached Wyatt's truck and took off. "The whole business of Melissa Reiver and her brother has finally been buried forever. You're looking at a new man with big plans."

"I sense another wedding coming up."

Porter nodded. "As soon as Lily is well enough to walk down the aisle."

"That's the best news ever."

His lips quirked. "All the wives can stop trying to set me up with a special woman who'll be perfect for me."

"I still haven't met Lily yet. How come?"

"I was keeping her under wraps during my therapy for fear you guys would give me too hard a time."

"So she's hot," Wyatt mused.

"You have no idea."

The other man laughed. "Really."

"I promise you'll meet her in a few days when I drive her home."

"Can't wait."

It was evening by the time they turned into the drive winding into the Owens ranch. They'd stopped for some fast-food tacos on the way since they were both famished.

"My car's over by the corral. Can't thank you enough for the lift, Wyatt."

"What are friends for?" He pulled up to it.

Porter opened the truck door, but before he got out, he paused. "If there'd never been a Melissa Reiver hunting me down, I wouldn't be living in the Wind River Mountain Range with friends like you or have met the love of my life."

"I hear you," Wyatt murmured. "As you know, years ago when my parents and brother were killed by lightning in Nebraska, I had to come live with my grandparents here. I was in so much pain back then, I couldn't imagine being happy again. Then Alex showed up at the sheep camp and I felt reborn."

"Holden told me a similar story. After losing his wife to cancer, his agony was so bad, his parents urged him to leave Cody and take the sheriff job here. A couple of years later, Jessica showed up in his office on a case and transformed his world."

After getting out of the truck, he turned to Wyatt. "When you think about it, Cole's the only homegrown guy. Ironic he had to spend so many years away before coming back to claim Tamsin."

Wyatt nodded. "Life is good. We're going to throw you an engagement party on my ranch as soon as Lily is mobile."

"First I need to propose to her, but I like the sound of that. Thanks again for everything."

Porter closed the door and got in his car. Before he showed up at the hospital, he needed to go home to shower and change clothes since he planned to spend the night with Lily. He also needed to get to a florist for some flowers.

Chapter 10

Lily's parents were at her bedside and had eaten the dinner the kitchen had sent up for them. She still had the IV in her arm and would be on fluids until morning. They'd propped her leg, making it awkward for her to sit up.

While they talked about Trixie's care, she heard a tap on the door and her blond-headed hero came in her hospital room with a vase of red roses. She gasped in delight. The sight of him freshly shaven in a sport shirt and chinos stole her breath. As her mother had said earlier, he was one of the most handsome men she'd ever seen in her life. Her mom sure knew what she was talking about.

Porter set the flowers on the counter and walked over to kiss her lips, then greeted her parents. They talked for a few minutes. The crisis had created a closeness between the four of them. Though Lily was dying to be alone with him, she loved it that her folks were already crazy about Porter and wanted to hear any details he could share with them.

"I was on the phone with everyone on my drive over here. Holden contacted my old boss in New York to tell him the news." He stared into Lily's eyes. "Everyone is incredibly relieved and sends their best wishes for a quick and total recovery, sweetheart."

Her mother patted Porter's arm. "Now that you're here, we'll go."

"I've already talked to the desk and plan to spend the night with Lily. I promise to phone you if she needs or wants anything."

Her father smiled. "I think our Lily has everything she could ask for now that you've come. Good night, honey."

"I know you must be exhausted. Go home and get some sleep." Lily kissed her parents.

"We'll call you in the morning."

"Thanks for everything, Mom."

Porter walked them to the door and they said goodnight.

"I thought you'd never get here," she said softly.

He rushed over to her. "I'm sorry it took this long," he whispered against her lips. "Because it was a criminal case, I had to stop at police headquarters to make official statements and clarify the facts while everything was fresh."

"I understand, darling."

Darling. The most beautiful word he'd ever heard.

His eyes searched every centimeter of her features. "Your color has come back. Honestly, Lily, you're so gorgeous, and I'm so thankful you're alive, I'm close to speechless. Just let me hold you for a minute."

He pulled her close to him, breaking down her last barrier, and she wept softly in his arms. They stayed that way until housekeeping came in with his cot.

After the man had gone back out, she groaned because Porter separated himself from her long enough to set the cot next to her bed on the other side, away from the computer. She watched him in the semidarkness.

"I've dreamed about us sleeping together, Porter, but never imagined our first night would be like this."

He came close again and propped himself on the edge of her bed with both arms spread on either side of her shoulders. "Tell me about it."

"Where did you go after you left the hospital earlier?"

"Wyatt drove me to pick up my car."

"That's right. It was parked by the corral."

"Yup. The two of us got a bite to eat before I went home to do everything else. We both agreed that true life is stranger than fiction. You and I met under highly unusual circumstances, and there's been nothing normal about our relationship ever since."

"I wouldn't have had it any other way."

"Except for the Reiver family, neither would I. But they're out of our lives now." He leaned down and kissed her passionately until she moaned with pleasure.

Her eyes played over his face. "If you really want to know, helping you with your therapy thrilled me from the very start."

He smiled. "Since we're comparing notes, on that first day when you put that gait belt around me, I came close to grabbing you and kissing you senseless. The only thing that stopped me was the fear that you'd slap me and order me to leave. I couldn't risk that when I'd just found you."

"You hid your feelings so well, I went crazy."

"I loved you immediately. It happened so hard and fast, I forgot all about my accident and was determined to win your love no matter how long it took." He tenderly cradled her face in his hands. "Now that I know you love me, too, I want to make love to you all night.

"But once again, we can't be alone together in here the way I want any more than we could have made love on the pad of the therapy-room floor yesterday. You have to hurry and get better, or I'm going to be climbing the walls. A man can only take so much."

"Women have the same problem," she admitted and kissed him hungrily, though she was starting to have trouble staying awake. Once again, his kisses whisked her away to a divine place, where nothing mattered but to love and be loved. "Please don't move," she begged when he started to sit up.

"We can't do this, sweetheart. It's after eleven. You need to rest. I'm going to get on the cot and be with you all night. We'll talk until your pain meds put you to sleep."

"Promise you'll stay right here?"

He quirked an eyebrow. "What do *you* think?"

"I think I'm so insanely in love with the most fantastic ranger in the Winds, I don't know myself anymore."

"I can tell you're feeling the medication, but I love hearing anything you have to say." One more kiss and he slid off the edge of her bed. After fixing the cot blanket and pillow, he lay down and turned on his side toward her. "Can you see me?"

She chuckled. "Kind of, but you're too far away."

"Our time is coming."

"I can't wait!"

Suddenly the door opened and a nurse came in to check her vital signs and the IV bag. "You two have been on the news tonight and are full-blown celebrities. Did you watch?"

Porter propped himself on one elbow. "No. We'd like to forget it."

The nurse logged information into the computer. "Well, I think you're both incredibly brave to have survived such a terrifying ordeal. If you need anything, just press that buzzer. I'm Doris, and I'm on duty all night."

"Thank you, Doris," Lily murmured. The minute the nurse left the room, Lily looked at the man she loved with all her heart and soul. "I didn't know we were on TV."

"According to Holden, it's the biggest story around here since he caught the killer of Jessica's first husband. A deranged brother and sister involved in high crime in these parts doesn't happen very often."

"Thank heaven." Lily shivered. "Isn't it tragic and sad that they grew up so disturbed?"

"It is, but I'd like to change the subject. Did your folks have news on Trixie?"

"Yes. The vet said she got grazed on her upper limb

over the fleshy muscle part and will heal quickly, but she might have a scar."

"Just like you," he murmured. "I'm sure she's missing you. But you'll both be together before long."

"Poor Dash."

"We can be thankful he wasn't injured. One of the deputies rode him back to the ranch."

"All those men protecting us were so brave, Porter. How do we thank them?"

He winked. "I have some ideas, but they'll keep for tomorrow."

"I…can't wait until…morning…"

Lily was still sound asleep when Porter awakened at seven. He got off the cot and looked down at his black-haired sleeping beauty. Suppressing the urge to kiss her, he left the room and passed the nursing station. Doris was still on duty.

"I need to freshen up. If Lily wakes up before I'm back, tell her I'm still in the hospital and will join her shortly."

She nodded. "I'm going off duty now, but I'll tell Georgia, the day nurse."

"Thank you."

He headed downstairs. After visiting the restroom, he bought a quick breakfast in the cafeteria and phoned his mother again.

"Darling—how's Lily this morning?"

"As far as I could tell, she had a peaceful night. I'm going back to her room in a few minutes, but first I have some more news for you."

"What? That you're madly in love? You think I don't know that? I prayed this day would come."

His eyes closed tightly. "I didn't think it would, but now everything has changed and I want to marry her as soon as she's recovered enough to make it through a wedding. Of course I have to propose first, but I want you to be thinking ahead. Look at Art's schedule so you can plan to fly out here. Naturally you'll be staying at the ranch."

"What time frame are you thinking?"

"Tomorrow," he teased, except that he wasn't joking. He could only wish it was tomorrow.

"Porter—"

"I'd say three weeks to a month. We haven't made plans yet and we have to talk to her folks, too. You're going to like them a lot. As for Lily, you're going to be crazy about her."

"I don't doubt that," his mom said. "Art just left for work, but I'll phone him and tell him the great news. I'll admit I'm dying to fly out there and see where you live."

"Better be careful. You might like it so much, you'll want to move here. What I'd give to have you near us to share in our lives."

His mother choked up. "I'd do it in a minute, but Art's business is here."

"I know, but I can dream a little."

"Before we hang up, how's your back?" his mom asked.

He grinned. "To be honest, I'm in great shape and have forgotten all about it, thanks to Lily's expertise."

"That's wonderful. Can I tell you again how thankful I am that you and Lily are alive and have a future to look forward to?"

"Thanks, Mom. Love you."

He hung up and hurried back to Lily's room, but he was told to wait in the hall until her dressing had been changed. Ron saw him standing outside her door.

"Hey—you guys are famous!" He shook Porter's hand. "I'm glad you're both okay."

"Me, too."

"So...are you two...?"

"Yup."

"The first time I wheeled you down to the clinic, I figured something was going to happen. Sure enough, when I entered the therapy room to pick you up and saw the way the two of you looked at each other, I knew you were both goners. I'll admit I was jealous."

Laughter burst from Porter. "Thanks for all your help."

While they talked, the door opened and the nurse named Georgia came out. "You can go in now, Mr. Ewing. She's been asking for you."

Ron winked at him before walking off.

The second he entered the room he noticed two things. The IV was gone, and the head of Lily's bed had been propped enough that she didn't have to lie flat. "Porter—"

He rushed over and kissed her, wishing he could crush her in his arms. By the way she was kissing him back, he could tell she felt better. "You look too beautiful for someone who's been shot in the leg."

She cupped his face in her hands. "Have I ever told

you that every time I see you, my heart turns over on itself and I can hardly breathe?"

Everything she said and did enchanted him. "Are you really feeling as good as you look, sweetheart? What about your leg pain?"

"It's not that bad."

"What about that part of your spine."

"I wasn't hurt there. Stop worrying. Now that we're both alive and there's no more threat to our happiness, I'm literally floating."

Just then the door opened and the nurse wheeled the bed top over her. "Your breakfast is on its way. Soft foods and drinks today."

"I'm ready for real food."

"Tell the doctor when he does his rounds this evening."

No sooner had she gone out than Lily was brought a tray with Jell-O, toast and juice. "That looks good," Porter commented.

"We should ask them to bring you a tray."

He shook his head. "I already ate in the cafeteria while I talked to my mother again."

Lily drank her juice and started munching on her toast. "I bet she's dying to see you."

"She wanted to fly out immediately, but I told her to wait until the wedding." He stared into her eyes. "I'm asking you now because I can't wait any longer. Will you marry me, Lily? Be my wife and the mother of our children? Just as soon as possible? There's nothing standing in our way."

She didn't answer him immediately. Instead she put

the rest of her toast back on the plate. That's when he got his first inkling that something was wrong. But how could anything be wrong? "Sweetheart?"

Tears filled her eyes, but they didn't fall. "You know how much I love you, and there's nothing more I want than to say yes, but we have to talk seriously before I give you an answer. I mean *really* seriously."

In a heartbeat he started to feel ill. "Does this have anything to do with the man you'd planned to marry eight years ago?"

"No, darling. This has to do with me and my body."

"I don't understand."

"When I told you what happened to my spine after the crash, and the possibility of paralysis if I tried to ski again, the doctor also told me something else."

What she didn't say hit him like a blow to the gut. "Are you saying you can't have children?"

"No. The damage didn't do anything like that. But when I asked him that question, he did say pregnancy might bring on paralysis. He didn't get into any details, and I was so hysterical at the time over Steve's deception, I was in no frame of mind to listen to what he had to tell me. Nothing seemed to matter then."

Porter was trying to take it all in.

"I didn't really think about marriage and children until I met you and found myself dreaming about a future with you and the family I wanted to have with you."

He pulled up a chair and sat down next to her. "So why don't we get your doctor in Salt Lake City on the phone and ask him for that detailed explanation you couldn't bear to talk about eight years ago? As soon as you're better, we could fly to Utah and have a consultation with him, look at your X-rays."

She reached out so he'd take her hand. "We'll do it as soon as I can get around on crutches because I want to marry you and have a family. But we'd better not set a date yet."

Porter groaned inwardly. "Tell me the truth. Is that because you've decided you won't marry me if you can't give me a child without risk? I want *you*, Lily. If having a baby would put you in danger, we won't let it happen."

"Listen to me, Porter. The possibility of not being able to give you a child is unthinkable to me. You deserve to be a father."

"No one deserves to be anything," he said in a quiet voice. "We make our own lives. You and I will handle whatever we have to once we talk to your doctor and get his expert advice on everything. But right now, I'm asking you to marry me."

"Porter—" Her voice shook. "What I'm asking is that we don't make any decisions until after I've seen him. Within a month we'll have answers."

Upset because he knew Lily was a self-sacrificing person, he got to his feet and paced the floor, crushed by this new obstacle. All he'd done was think about a future with her from the moment they'd met, not realizing she'd been living with this fear.

"I'm sorry for acting so upset, sweetheart. Of course, we'll wait until you see the doctor. I've never been in love before. Forgive me?"

She started to answer him but her parents came in the room with the nurse, who was carrying more flowers. They hurried over to her while Georgia put the daisies on the counter.

Porter grabbed the edge of the chair to steady himself and get a grip on his emotions.

"You haven't finished your breakfast, Ms. Owens."

Lily pasted on a smile for the nurse's sake. "I'm still working on it."

"Good. You need the liquid."

Porter smiled at her parents and moved closer to the bed. "Since your folks are here, I have some errands to run, then I'll be back and plan to spend the rest of the day and night with you."

Her eyes filled with anxiety. "I'll be waiting. Don't be too long."

Porter pressed a kiss to her lips, said goodbye to her folks and hurried out of the room. He should have been able to handle it when she'd told him they would have to put their marriage plans on hold until after she'd been examined. How insensitive could he be when she was just recovering from a gunshot wound?

All this time she'd been suffering over the condition of her spine and what effect pregnancy would have on her. He'd had no idea.

Porter wanted to make it up to her for upsetting her. He knew one thing he could do to let her know how much he loved her. After leaving the hospital, he drove downtown to RK Jewelers and asked to be shown some diamonds. The young woman who waited on him couldn't have been more helpful.

"I want a round, one-carat blue-white diamond with

two round half-carat amethysts on either side of it set in white gold."

She found the desired stones for him to examine and placed them on a piece of black velvet.

"These are exactly what I want. How soon could you have this ring ready for me? I'm in a hurry."

"What's her size?" the saleswoman asked.

"Probably the same as yours."

"Our jeweler could have it ready by five o'clock. Would that do?"

"Perfect. Could you courier the package to this address?" He wrote instructions for it to be taken to the nursing station on the third-floor surgical wing of Whitebark Hospital. "I'll inform the medical staff to expect a package for me."

"We'll be happy to take care of that for you. Whoever receives this knockout ring is a lucky woman."

"*I'm* the lucky one, but thank you for your help."

He handed her his credit card and within five minutes he left the store. Before he returned to the hospital, he drove to headquarters for a talk with Stan about buying Dash.

Tomorrow Porter would drive over to the Owens ranch with his horse trailer and get him moved. After being able to mount him without a stool, Porter knew he was ready to get back to his forest-ranger work and told Stan as much.

No more filling out papers for the department. He needed to be outdoors doing the job he was hired for. But until he and Lily had flown to Salt Lake City for a medical consultation, he wanted an assignment where he could be back in town every evening to be with her.

He stopped at his ranch long enough to shower and change clothes. After eating a couple of sandwiches, he left for the hospital. Now that he'd made his purchase, he'd calmed down enough to do this thing right and show her he loved her beyond all else and would be patient.

Once again patience was the key.

On the way to her room, he met her parents in the hall. "How is she doing this afternoon?" It was ten after four. He'd been gone a little longer than he'd planned, but his errand had been worth it.

"She's fine, but missing you," her father said. "We have to get back to the ranch. A client is coming."

"I'm sorry I didn't get here sooner, but I had to stop at work to talk with my boss. I've made arrangements to pick up Dash tomorrow."

"He's a great horse for you."

"Lily convinced me of that before I ever rode him," he confided. "Now that I'm back at the hospital, I'll stay again tonight."

"Lily will be thrilled."

"She puts on a good show, but you know your daughter better than anyone. Is she being honest about telling us she's not in pain?"

Caroline and Ross nodded at the same time. Her mother put a hand on his arm. "Her pain has more to do with you and the dreadful turmoil that ranger put you through."

"You know something, Caroline? If it hadn't happened, Lily and I would never have met. I can't comprehend life without her."

"Well, the feeling is definitely mutual on her part. We'll talk to you tomorrow."

From their demeanor, Porter didn't think Lily had told them anything about their conversation and his proposal before he'd left her room earlier. It was just as well. He wondered if her parents knew of this other fear that pregnancy might bring on paralysis.

He walked them to the elevator before he headed back to her room and paused at the nursing station.

"A package for me is being couriered here sometime after five. Would you let me know when it has arrived?"

"Of course."

After reaching her room, he knocked on the door the way a certain orderly used to do.

"Ron? Is that you? Come in."

"Sorry if you're disappointed, sweetheart. It's only me." More flowers had been delivered, decorating the room.

"Oh," she cried. "You big tease. I'm so glad you're back. What took you so long?"

"Things."

"I was afraid I'd upset you by asking you to wait before we make wedding plans. I'm worried you'll never be able to forgive me."

He walked over to the bed and cradled her face in his hands. "I'm the one who should apologize for getting upset. I'm so crazy about you, Lily, I didn't want to hear about anything that could keep us apart. It was wrong of me, especially when I didn't know how worried you've been all these years."

"It was my fault. I should have explained everything when I first told you about my skiing accident."

"I was a stranger to you then. Why would you have?"

"Will you forgive me?"

"Oh, Lily—"

Their mouths met in a frenzy of want. When they both needed to take a breath, he lifted his head. "Why don't we call your doctor and make an appointment?"

"You mean now?"

"Why not. We may be able to catch him if he's still at his office. What's his name?"

"Dr. David Gregson. He works at the university hospital in Salt Lake City."

Porter pulled up the chair by her bed and sat down to make the call. He was put through to reception and handed it to Lily. He listened while she explained her reason for phoning.

It was clear that the doctor wasn't there, disappointing Porter. After a minute she hung up and handed back his phone.

"His receptionist told me he's out of the country. She scheduled me for an appointment on July seventeenth, when he's back in his office."

Three weeks away sounded like an eternity, but he'd learned his lesson earlier today and would wait for as long as it took. "I'm glad it's made," he murmured before kissing her again, pressing her back against the pillow. But, in time, no kiss was long enough or deep enough to satisfy either of them.

A rap sounded on the door, and a staff person called to him, causing him to lift his head. "There's a message for you at the front desk, Mr. Ewing."

"Thank you." Overjoyed the package had arrived, he eased away from Lily. "I'll be right back."

"I wonder why you weren't called on your cell phone."

"I don't know, but I'm going to find out."

He left the room and walked down the hall to the nursing station, where he was handed a padded envelope. Before returning to the room, he opened it and pulled out the little velvet box.

Even *he* let out a slight gasp at the beauty of the stones when he lifted the lid. Then he shut the box and put it in his shirt pocket. Turning to the person on duty, he asked, "Do you have a wastebasket?"

"Sure." She took the envelope from him.

With a nod of thanks he hurried back to Lily.

"What was that about?" she asked the second he walked in.

He found a spot on the edge of her bed, then pulled the little black velvet box out of his shirt pocket. "For one thing, I should never have asked you to marry me without giving you this first."

When she saw it, she put a hand to her mouth. He opened the box for her.

"Oh, Porter…" she breathed. "That's the most exquisite engagement ring I've ever seen in my life." When she looked at him, her moist eyes outshone the amethysts.

"Let me put it on you to make this official, even if we can't pick a date yet."

Her lower lip trembled. "But I haven't seen the doctor yet, and—"

"No buts, Lily," he interjected. "We're getting married. This is it. What we have is too precious to let anything get in the way. If we can't have a baby without doing damage, then we'll figure out something else, but we're in this forever. I want you for my wife *forever*. Do you hear me?"

He reached for her left hand to slide it home on her ring finger, but she pulled back, shocking him to the core of his being.

"I can't let you give this to me. Not yet. One day you could live to regret it."

Pain welled up inside of him. He got to his feet, clutching the ring in his hand. He'd been wrong to think a ring would help to reassure her that he wanted her under any conditions.

"You're rejecting me without even seeing your doctor first?"

"Because… I know what he's going to say."

Porter shook his head. "You really believe the worst, don't you? It appears the man you planned to marry years ago did more damage to your psyche than I realized. I thought we understood each other, but I was wrong."

Tears rolled down her cheeks. "You don't understand, Porter."

"Oh, yes, I do. You don't have enough faith in me, in us! Whatever happened to us working through this together? We love each other, but apparently my love can't overcome the insurmountable in your eyes."

"No, darling. That's not true."

"I'm afraid it is, otherwise this ring would be on your finger." He forced his next words out through clenched teeth. "I need some time to think, so I'm going to leave."

"Oh, please, Porter, don't go."

"It's for the best," he said. "When I get out to the car, I'll call your parents and tell them an emergency came up and I couldn't stay with you overnight after all. I'm sure they'll understand and come back to be with you."

Without another word, he strode out the door.

Chapter 11

Three weeks later a devastated Lily flew to Salt Lake City with her mother for her exam with Dr. Gregson. By now she didn't need her crutches and walked reasonably well, but twenty-one long, empty days without seeing or talking to Porter had been like a death sentence.

She knew she'd hurt him terribly. But to condemn him to a wife who might live out her life in a wheelchair by giving him a child she knew he wanted would be beyond cruel. Any woman would sell her soul to be married to a man like Porter, especially one who could bear him children without problem. She still felt he should be given that option.

Both her parents were silent on the matter because they thought the world of Porter. That was okay. This decision was Lily's, and hers alone.

After a morning of testing and X-rays, the doctor asked her to come in to his office alone so they could talk. When she entered it, she was reminded of their conversation years earlier, when she'd heard what he'd told her, but hadn't really listened.

"Lily? You've come a long way since you were flown in from Vancouver. You've made an enviable career for yourself and show no physical signs of the injury to your spine. I'm impressed you're recovering so well from that gunshot wound. Anyone knowing your history would say you're a great success story.

"But I don't see a ring on your finger and have to admit that surprises me. A beautiful woman like you must have a string of admirers. So I sense there's something you haven't told me. What's the real reason you came for an exam after all this time?"

She sat back in the chair. "Three weeks ago the man I love gave me an engagement ring, but I couldn't put it on."

He frowned. "Why is that?"

For the next ten minutes she unloaded to him, telling him everything and revealing her fears. "I purposely didn't tell you why I wanted this appointment because I needed to hear your honest assessment about my injury. Has anything about my condition changed or grown worse? Are you still of the opinion that if I got pregnant, it could mean paralysis?"

"If that's what you thought I said, then it means you didn't hear everything I told you the first time because you were in such a bad way after your crash. I remember your being terrified that you couldn't ski or have a baby."

Lily sat forward in surprise. "I know I was, and admit I can't recall everything you said to me."

"Then let me clarify some points for you and answer one of your questions first. After today's examination and a thorough look at the X-ray, I find that you've healed even better than I'd hoped.

"As for getting pregnant, I saw no reason why you couldn't have a baby then or now. What you don't remember is this—I told you that in the latter stages of pregnancy, the baby might put pressure on that traumatized area. But if that were the case, your obstetrician would do a cesarean section before any damage could be done. In other words, I believe you can have several children with no fear at all."

"You told me all that?" Lily was incredulous to realize how hysterical she'd been after her crash. *Oh, my heavens! What have I done to Porter?*

He nodded. "I had no idea you've been living with that anxiety all this time. As I recall, you were working with a psychiatrist."

"Yes, but I never told him about fears. We talked about possible careers for me."

"What a shame," he murmured. "Certainly it's true that training to ski again wouldn't have been wise in case you were subjected to another severe fall. I'm glad for your sake you stayed away from the sport.

"But as for having a baby and being a mother, that's entirely different. What I would advise at this stage is for you to visit with your obstetrician right away and tell him or her your history. If you choose to marry and should become pregnant, then you'll be under close supervision with all the latest modern advantages. Go home to this man you love and enjoy your life!"

Her heart pounded in her throat as she got up from the chair. "I plan to! Thank you, Dr. Gregson. You've made a new woman of me!"

She hurried out of his office. Her mother stood up when she saw her coming. "I've been a mess, Mom, and have made every mistake in the book. I'll tell you all about it in the rental car on the way to the airport. I have to get home to Porter as fast as possible."

"Your father will be meeting us in Jackson Hole," her mother reminded her. "We have reservations to stay there until tomorrow."

"That's right."

Lily was going to have to live through another twelve hours before she could find Porter and talk to him. She could try calling him on the phone, but she knew in her heart he wouldn't respond. This wasn't something to be discussed over the phone, anyway. Anything this earth-shaking had to be done in person and would probably take a long time considering how deeply she'd hurt him, but she'd never give up. *Never.*

Yesterday was the day Lily was supposed to have seen Dr. Gregson in Salt Lake City.

Porter's watch alarm went off at 5:30 a.m. every morning while he was in the mountains. But this morning he'd awakened to that thought.

There were always messages from his friends and

several from his mother on his cell phone. He texted them back to let them know he was alive, but in three weeks there'd been no contact from Lily and he was empty inside.

Since coming up here with Dash, he hadn't been back to town since. The fact that Lily had seen the doctor yesterday—*if* she'd seen him at all without leaving Porter a response—spoke volumes.

Why he kept looking for her to contact him meant he was delusional. She'd turned him down for reasons that made sense to her and he had to accept them for the sake of his sanity.

A few days ago Martin had called him to talk. He said he still wanted him back in the Adirondacks if he ever changed his mind.

Why not transfer again?

Porter knew he'd never get over Lily. Though he had great friends, to stay here would be too painful knowing she lived in the same town. The more he thought about it, the more the idea of leaving Wyoming sounded like the only thing to do if he wanted to get on with his life.

He climbed out of his sleeping bag like a robot and got ready for his job. With the beautiful weather holding, the forest below Glimpse Lake was filled with fishermen and campers, many of whom disobeyed the rules. By the end of the day he imagined he'd have given out a dozen fines and would most likely would have had to deal with bikers who liked to blaze their own illegal trail off the fire break roads.

This evening he'd drive back to town and contact the Realtor he'd used to buy the ranch here and ask him to put it back on the market. Tomorrow morning he'd go to headquarters and tell Stan he was flying back to New York ASAP. His boss would understand and arrange the transfer with Martin. As for Dash, Porter would ask Cole to return him to the Owens ranch. All these thoughts and more filled his head as he went about his business.

At four that afternoon he returned to his camping spot and packed everything in his truck. After he'd loaded Dash in the trailer, he headed down the mountain, eager to put things in motion.

By five thirty he drove around the back of his ranch to the barn. He fed and watered his horse, then headed for the house. It occurred to him he'd be following in his father's footsteps. Once his parents had divorced, Porter's dad left the family home to live on his own until he died because he'd only loved Porter's mother.

Porter had inherited his genes because he, too, could only devote himself to one woman.

He reached for his duffel bag and pulled out his keys, but the back door opened before he could unlock it. When he saw who stood there, he thought he was hallucinating.

Lily...

"Please don't be upset that I'm here, Porter. Cole told me you were still up in the mountains and might not come back down for a while. But he let me in to wait when I told him this was an emergency. I've been here since I got back from Jackson Hole."

"Jackson Hole?" His mind had to be playing tricks on him.

"Yes. Mother and I flew there from Salt Lake City yesterday evening. Dad met us and we spent the night at a hotel. This morning he brought us home. I packed some of my things and planned to stay here until you showed up, whenever that was. You and I need to have the most serious talk of our lives."

He had trouble breathing. "We already did that." Porter entered the kitchen and shut the door, then plunked his bag on the floor.

She shook her head. "No. I wouldn't let you and made it so impossible, you had no choice but to leave my hospital room. I don't know if you'll ever be able to forgive me for the way I behaved."

Porter turned on the cold-water tap and drank from it for a long time before looking at her. "There's nothing to forgive, Lily. I had no idea you'd been harboring that secret for such a long time. When I first met you, I couldn't figure out why some lucky guy hadn't snapped you up a long time ago. The reason is no longer a mystery. I don't like anything about your decision, but I respect you and, oddly enough, admire you."

"What do you mean?"

"For having the guts to turn me down when I proposed. Like I told you once, you're the bravest woman I know. That bravery, no matter how misguided, has helped me make a decision."

She rubbed the sides of her curvy, jean-clad hips with her hands. "What decision?"

He folded his arms across his chest. "I'm leaving Wyoming, hopefully by tomorrow evening."

Her beautiful face crumbled. "Wh-where are you going?" she stammered.

"Back home. Melissa Reiver is no longer a threat, and Martin is ready to give me back my old job."

Her eyes widened. "You *want* to leave?" She sounded heartbroken, but how was that possible?

"Surely you realize that *want* has nothing to do with it. A door has been closed to me. Instead of destroying myself attempting to pry it open, I'd prefer to move on."

She bit her lower lip. "You don't have to do anything. It's already open to you and only you."

"Is this some kind of riddle?"

"You know it's not." Pain edged her breathtaking features. "What I'm trying to say is, I want to be your wife and I'll marry you anytime you say. If you'll put that ring on my finger, it will never come off."

Porter couldn't take much more. "That's interesting. Am I to deduce that the doctor told you a miracle has happened since your crash, and now you can have my baby without worry that I'll be stuck with a wheelchair-bound wife?"

Tears filled her eyes. "In a word, *yes*."

That word permeated the kitchen and infiltrated his body, stunning him.

"Tell me the truth."

"Dr. Gregson gave me a physical yesterday morning, complete with X-rays. When he talked to me after, I asked him if anything about my condition had changed or grown worse. He said I'd healed even better than he'd hoped and saw no reason why I couldn't have a baby now. So I asked, what if the pregnancy brings on paralysis, like he'd once intimated? He was surprised to realize that I truly hadn't taken in everything he'd told me before."

Maybe Porter was dreaming. "Go on."

"When I was brought in, I was convinced my life was over. No more skiing, no hope for children one day." She took a breath. "During my hysteria, evidently I didn't hear him tell me the most important news."

"What would that have been?"

"That the crash didn't ruin my ability to safely carry a baby to term. What he did tell me was that in the latter stages of pregnancy, the baby might put pressure on the traumatized area of my spine."

Maybe Porter was hearing things.

"In the worst-case scenario, my obstetrician would do a cesarean section before any damage could be done. In other words, he told me I could have several children with no fear at all. I'll be able to give you a son and a daughter, whatever comes first. But I had been in such a bad way back then, I didn't listen."

He was still in shock, trying to compute. "Do you have an obstetrician?"

"Yes. Dr. Gregson told me to make an appointment right away with a Dr. Sharp here in Whitebark and tell him my whole history. He said these days there's new technology and more advances in this field to make certain my spine doesn't suffer. I want us to go together so we both hear everything at the same time."

He cocked his head. "Knowing your history, I think that might be a good idea."

Lily's face was bathed in tears as she pulled a man's

gold band from her pocket. "Oh, darling—will you marry me?" She rushed toward him and grabbed his left hand to put the band on his ring finger.

He couldn't believe this was happening.

"We'll have the most beautiful life. Just don't turn me down. Please give me the chance I didn't give you. That was my fault. Maybe one day you can forgive my cruelty."

"If you were cruel, it was because you were trying to spare me future grief." He pulled her close and pressed his forehead against hers. "That kind of sacrifice only makes me love you more, even if I had to run to the mountains to deal with my pain."

"If you didn't come home by tomorrow, I planned to find where you were camping and join you."

The love illuminating those lavender eyes compelled Porter to sweep her up in his arms and carry her to his bedroom.

"Darling—" She let out a cry. "You shouldn't be lifting me yet."

He flashed her a smile. "I've had three weeks to recover and am no longer a patient. What about your wound?"

"It's healing just fine and no infection."

"Thank heaven."

When he reached the room, he lowered her to the bed, but didn't join her. "Don't move. I need to get something out of the drawer."

"I'm not going anywhere," she whispered.

"No, you're not, because *this* means we belong to each other."

He leaned over long enough to put the ring on her finger before joining her. "Can you believe we're not in the clinic or your hospital room? Just in case you were worrying, I don't need a therapist to show me how to love you the way I'm dying to do. I have my own moves. Give me that luscious mouth of yours, sweetheart."

"I love you so terribly," she cried. "You're my everything. I'll spend the rest of my life showing you what you mean to me."

Their hunger knew no bounds. Porter had already forgiven her for the pain she'd caused. Lily couldn't show him enough how much she loved him. She had no idea how much time had passed while they got swept up in the heat of the moment, but when he suddenly eased himself away from her and stood up, her heart sank.

"What's wrong, darling?"

"We can't do this. I want our first time to happen on our wedding night, after we've been to visit your OB. There's no such a thing as being too careful when it comes to your health."

Lily wanted to argue with him, but decided she'd better keep quiet after what she'd put him through. Besides, she wouldn't win this argument. When he dug in his heels, that was it. So it appeared she would have to wait because she was going to marry the most magnificent ranger this side of the Continental Divide.

Taking a deep breath, she rolled off the other side of the bed and stood up to slip into her sandals. "When was the last time you ate?" She knew he had to be starving.

"I don't remember." He sounded grumpy now that he'd delivered his edict.

"I don't suppose you have food in the fridge after being gone so long. Why don't we both freshen up. I'll take the bathroom down the hall. When we're ready, let's go out for a fabulous dinner to celebrate our engagement and make wedding plans. I want to show off my fiancé and my ring."

He grabbed her around the waist and kissed her with such passion, her legs almost gave out. "You have no idea how much I love you."

"A minute ago I was starting to believe you," she teased. "I guess you'll have to finish convincing me after we take our vows. The sooner, the better."

"Three weeks, no more."

"While we're at dinner, let's call your mother. I want to tell her that she raised the man of my dreams."

Porter tugged her close and kissed the back of her neck. "When I rode in earlier, I felt like my life was over."

"When I saw your truck out the window, I went through agony wondering if you would even speak to me. I had visions of being told to leave."

He hugged her even tighter against him. "That's all over, sweetheart. And for the record, I'm never letting you go."

A few minutes later Porter backed his car out of the garage and they left for town. On the way his cell phone rang. "It's Holden." He pulled into the right lane and turned a corner so he could stop in front of the first house. "He's going to be excited about our news." Porter clicked on. "Hey, bud?"

"Cole told me you were back and that Lily is with you. Put your phone on speaker so she can hear me, too."

Something was wrong. "Sure."

"Where are you?"

"In my car. We're on our way to dinner."

"You can't do that. Come to my office instead. Reiver's trial was held this morning. After sentencing he was transferred to the prison in Rawlins, but on the way he and another prisoner who'd been arrested for armed robbery escaped."

Lily's gasp resounded in the car.

"The police chief and I think the two of them came out to Wyoming with Melissa and that's how her brother was in the mountains without a car or horse. His partner would have provided the setup."

His hands gripped the wheel tighter. "That would explain a lot."

"I have no doubt they're coming back to finish what they started and have probably stashed weapons somewhere nearby. There's a massive manhunt on for them. In the meantime, I need to make plans with you and Lily."

"We'll be right there."

After he rang off, he turned to her. "I want you to put your head down as far as you can."

"All right."

He drove back to the highway and headed for the sheriff's office. Before long they arrived and he parked in one of the reserved spaces. "We're here. Let's get inside, sweetheart."

With his arm around her, they rushed in the building and hurried down the hallway to Holden's office.

"Thank God you're both all right," his friend said, telling them to sit down.

"Amen. Where did the escape happen?"

"Ten miles before the van reached Farson."

"What happened to the driver and the other deputy?" Porter asked.

"Both were shot, but they're stabilized and will make it."

Porter shook his head. "This just doesn't end. It means the others could have doubled back to Whitebark within the hour."

"Right. Two of the convicts were picked up on the other side of Farson."

"Unfortunately the wrong two got away," Porter muttered. "Reiver is a mean one in the worst sense of the word and has nothing to live for except to take me out."

"It's almost over," Holden murmured. "I take it you two are together now?"

They both held up their left hands, causing Holden to laugh. "That's the best news of the night. All we need to hear now is that the suspects have been caught. Then we're home-free. I've sent one of the guys to bring you some club sandwiches and coffee."

"Bless you, Holden."

"Do my parents know what's happened?"

"I phoned them the minute the news came in, Lily.

Their place has been searched and they're under surveillance as we speak."

"Thank you," she said, her voice trembling.

Porter clung to her hand. "How did they manage to escape?"

"There were four prisoners. Someone on the outside who knew the van's route forced the van off the road at gunpoint—it was all preplanned. The chief is arranging for protection for the two of you, but I wanted you here and safe while some deputies do a sweep of your house and ranch first."

"No one ever had a better friend." Only a few hours ago he'd been thinking of leaving Wyoming. But that was when he'd believed there was no hope.

One of the deputies came in with three sacks of food and coffee. Porter thanked him. After he left, Holden ate with them while he listened to dispatch for any news.

"When's the wedding?"

"Three weeks away, even if the whole wedding party has to be protected by the National Guard." More laughter rolled out of Holden. "I want my three buddies to stand in as my best man."

"We've been hoping for this day. How about the guys at the fire station to stand guard, too? My wife says you're the luckiest man in Wyoming to be involved with the famous Olympian, Lily Owens. I happen to agree. Shame on him for keeping you a secret from us since you met."

Porter sent his bride-to-be a loving glance. "I didn't know if she felt the same way."

Lily beamed. "You know darn well I fell so hard for you, I even got my hair cut so you'd notice."

"Oh, I noticed, sweetheart."

"Jessica and her mom are wonderful people, Holden. I've seen her and Chase many times at the salon when Millie does my hair. Once I almost asked her if she could tell me a little bit about Porter since he was a close friend of yours, but I never got up the nerve."

"She would have loved it. My wife is crazy about Porter. I'm thankful she didn't meet him first."

"That's bull and you know it," Porter muttered.

"Where are you two getting married?"

"We haven't talked about it yet," Lily answered, "but I'd like the ceremony to take place at our family's church, if it's all right with you, Porter."

He squeezed her hand. "What do you think?"

"I think I could be the happiest woman on earth if this nightmare were over. I thought it was…"

"It will be," Holden proclaimed in a solemn tone. "How's your leg, by the way? When you walked in, no one would know you'd been shot less than a month ago."

"It's healing with remarkable speed."

"I couldn't be happier for you." He sent Porter a glance. "I take it your back is okay now."

"Perfect, thanks to my stunning fiancée." He turned to her. "It's getting late. I'll drive you home with a police escort."

Holden nodded. "A surveillance team is outside waiting for you."

"But I don't want us to be separated." Her eyes pleaded with him.

"Sweetheart—I really need to be here until this standoff is over. Come on. You need to get to bed and elevate your leg."

With reluctance, she nodded and stood up. "Thank you for everything, Holden. I want everyone to stay safe."

"We all want that."

"I'll be back," he murmured to Holden before walking her out of the building to his car.

He drove to her ranch as fast as he could and still obeyed the speed limit. She phoned her parents that she'd be arriving in a few minutes. This time Porter parked in front of the ranch house and walked her up the steps of the front porch. Her parents opened the door and they all went inside.

"We're going to catch these men," he assured her parents. "I'm glad she's home safe. Now I have to leave."

"Wait, darling. Mom? Dad? I asked Porter to marry me tonight and he said yes. Show them your ring."

With a smile, Porter put out his left hand. "I'm wearing this until our wedding day and will only take it off long enough for her to put it back on my finger. She's wearing my ring and promised it would never come off."

"Welcome to the family!" her mother cried and hugged both of them. Then it was her father's turn. The emotional moment caused Porter's throat to swell, reminding him he needed to call his mother and tell her what had happened.

"Walk me to the door," he whispered to Lily, who clung to him. Before he opened it, he gave her a long, passionate kiss. "I know this will be over soon. Just hang on. I promise to call you all the time to give you updates."

"I can live with that. I just can't live without you."

Chapter 12

She wouldn't have to.

Porter hurried out to the car and drove back to Holden's office. En route he phoned his friend to see if there was any more news and learned that it was still only the two felons who had been captured. With that much good news, he called his mother and informed her of the latest development.

It took a lot of convincing to tell her things would be all right. Then he told her there was going to be a wedding in three weeks whether Reiver was still at large or not.

"I promise to stay in close touch. We'll see each other when you fly out. Love you, Mom."

Next, he phoned Lily, who answered on the first ring. "Has there been any news yet?"

"Nothing new."

"Which means Melissa's brother and accomplice are still at large."

"They can't be far and the deputies will nail them. Wait and see. I just got off the phone with my mother. I told her we're getting married in three weeks. I hope you've got your parents' calendar circled for three weeks because our plans are now in the works."

"It's done. We're talking to the pastor tomorrow and seeing about wedding invitations. Mom wants to do the reception at the house. How do you feel about that?"

"I love it. Tell your folks you're wearing *white*!"

Her gentle laughter thrilled him. "I'll convey your message so there's no misunderstanding."

"I want your parents' approval. Can you blame me?"

"Do you think I would? I love you more than ever for being such an honorable man. I wish I could have met your father."

"He would have loved you. Now get to bed. I'll call you first thing in the morning and we'll make plans to go get our marriage license. Good night, my love."

He clicked off. One more call needed to be made, but he'd phone Martin tomorrow. Porter hoped his old boss and his wife might be able to come to the wedding. Martin was the closest person he had to a father now.

"Coffee?" Holden asked after Porter arrived back at the sheriff's office.

"You've read my mind. Tell me what I can do right now."

"Nothing. Just stay here and keep me company."

"Your poor wife."

"Jessica's used to my hours. Chase wishes I worked at a bank, but he knows I'd hate it."

Porter chuckled. "I can't wait until Lily and I are married. I guess you don't know the reason why I took off for the mountains over the last three weeks."

"We've got time on our hands if you want to tell me."

For the next ten minutes he filled in his friend about Lily's history.

Holden sipped his coffee. "She's really been through it. I'm thankful you guys worked your way through your problem and found your way back to each other. Jessica and I had our problems when she told me she couldn't marry me."

"I knew something was wrong. What was the reason?"

Porter listened until Holden had finished.

"So she had a secret, too."

"Yup."

"Yet now you're expecting the child you thought you could never have." Porter winked at his friend. "It could come before my wedding."

"We're not sure."

"Well, in any event, I'm thrilled for you both."

Holden rolled his eyes. "I'd like to be thrilled for you. All we need to do is get Reiver and his cohort behind bars with no chance of his ever getting out. Their escape is a black mark on my record."

"Your record is spotless." Porter's eyes narrowed on him. "Evil will always be out there. You can't control everything."

"Thanks. I needed to hear that."

"Anytime."

They sat there through the night listening to the messages from the deputies phoning in. Every so often the police chief checked in with updates. The media had gotten hold of the news and the TV displayed pictures of the two convicts, who were still at large in the greater Whitebark area.

Porter got up to use the restroom. When he came back in at five thirty a.m., he found Holden on the phone. He motioned to Porter to come closer. There was an energy about him, alerting Porter that something significant was going down.

He didn't realize he was holding his breath until his friend hung up and shot to his feet. "They've been caught on the property on the east side of the Owens ranch. Gunfire was exchanged. Both culprits are wounded, but no officers were harmed."

"Hallelujah!"

"You can say that again." Holden gestured toward the door. "Get out of here, Porter. Tell your fiancée it's truly over."

"Now I'm going to give you an order. Go home to your wife and son."

"I'm heading out in a few. Walt's on his way in to take over."

"Talk to you later."

Porter flew down the hall and out to his car. Forgetting the speed limit, he reached Lily's house in record time. After he parked in front, he phoned her. She answered immediately.

"Porter? I've been awake half the night waiting to hear from you."

"It's over. They've been caught. I'm parked in front. Come out to the car. We'll drive to my ranch to take care of Dash and make breakfast while we work on our wedding plans three weeks from now."

At this point she broke down in tears of joy. She wasn't the only one.

August 9

"Lily and Porter? Since you've said your vows and pledged to love each unto death and beyond, I now pronounce you man and wife. You may kiss your bride."

Her heart thudded as she turned to receive his kiss. Lowering his mouth to hers, Porter swept her into his embrace and kissed her with such ardor, she got a little light-headed.

Throughout the four-o'clock ceremony at the church, Lily had been waiting for this moment. She was now Mrs. Porter Ewing, his wife. And this handsome, wonderful man was hers to love and cherish forever. Lily forgot they had an audience, and didn't want to let him go.

It was probably the longest kiss in history at the altar, but she didn't care. They were in front of all their friends and family. Their journey had been fraught with perils, but they'd survived and triumphed.

When they walked down the aisle and out to the front of the church, an amazing sight greeted them. Besides their dearest friends, a huge crowd had assembled. The women's horse brigade, a number of the firefighters on their truck, the police chief, Porter's boss, Stan, and many of the deputies and rangers on horseback were all there to clap and cheer, making their wedding day absolutely glorious.

If there was any shadow on the day, it couldn't possibly be called a shadow. Holden's absence from the altar with Cole and Wyatt meant that Jessica had gone into labor in the middle of the night. They just learned Holden was now the proud father of another son.

Both she and Porter were ecstatic over the news as they moved on to her ranch house for the reception. Everyone from the hospital and the clinic came, even some of Lily's favorite patients.

Porter's fantastic mother and her husband had arrived two days before and were helping Lily's parents. Martin Kroger and his wife were her parents' guests, too. They were all like one big happy family. After cutting the wedding cake, followed by dozens of toasts to the bride and groom, she changed out of her white-lace wedding dress and they left for Porter's ranch in his car.

They'd be spending the last two weeks of September in the Adirondacks. She wanted to see where he'd been born and lived. They would enjoy the sight of the full autumn foliage in blazing color. They'd also travel to Buffalo to stay with his mother and her husband for a few days before returning to Wyoming.

For now they just wanted to enjoy married life and soak up the joy of being together at last, free from all worry.

Porter drove them around the back and carried her

over the threshold into his house. They never stopped kissing as he walked her through the kitchen and down the hall to his bedroom.

Someone had been here earlier. There were flowers and champagne on ice. She didn't care for alcohol, but loved whoever had gone to the trouble to make their bedroom a haven of love.

He helped her off with her suit jacket. "I'm so glad I don't have to undo all the buttons on the back of your wedding dress. You've made this divinely easy for me."

"I did it on purpose. I'm as impatient as you are."

This time Porter followed her down on the bed and the world faded away as they became one.

When Lily came awake, it was close to nine o'clock in the morning. Her husband was finally down for the count. They'd made love over and over again during the night. She'd been breathless with ecstasy.

Just looking at him made her want to start the whole process again and never stop. She raised up on one elbow and kissed his face, loving every male inch of him. He'd been tender, yet masterful, titillating her in ways she couldn't have imagined.

Lily already loved married life. Her only worry now was how she was going to handle it when he had to get up and go work. But he wouldn't be going to work for several days, so she needed to stop thinking and just bask in the wonderment of being his wife.

She traced his profile with her index finger. He was a beautiful man and she imagined there'd been many women who'd wanted a relationship with him.

But somehow she'd been the lucky one. Her mind kept going back to that first day in the clinic.

Sharon Carter had brought Lily a new patient complete with his file and X-rays. "He came in on an emergency. Nothing's broken, but he'll need therapy. A word to the wise. He's upset to have to be in here," she whispered. "Have fun, anyway." Her eyes had danced.

That last remark needed no explanation when Lily saw the strikingly handsome forest ranger for the first time. Like a thunderclap her heart had sprung to life and she hadn't been the same since.

"What's that secret smile for?"

Lily blinked. She hadn't realized Porter was awake. He rolled toward her and gave her a lingering kiss that lit her body on fire all over again.

"I was remembering the first morning I met you."

"If you want to know the truth, I'll never forget it, either. I decided you were a goddess come to life."

"Porter." She hid her face in his shoulder.

"It's true. I couldn't believe I hadn't seen you around town before. Every man who worked with you was under your spell. The hardest thing I had to do was wait for my one hour with you three times a week. Talk about torture."

"Shall we compare notes?" She kissed his mouth over and over again. "Every time Ron wheeled you out of the room, my heart literally sank. I went crazy waiting for the hours and days to pass between sessions."

"He knew I was crazy about you."

"Not much gets past Ron. I even drove to a medical conference that first weekend in Jackson Hole to help me deal with the fact that I wanted to spend time with you in your hospital room. Imagine the gossip that would have created."

He flashed her a grin. "If you'd come to see me, I would probably have had a heart attack."

"What about now?"

"I think you know exactly what you do to me. I love you, Lily. I love you," he growled in a low, savage voice and started to devour her.

Once again they lost track of time while they brought each other to the height of exquisite, soul-shattering pleasure.

When she next became aware of her surroundings, Porter's leg was wrapped around hers, and he was staring at her with an intense expression on his face.

"What is it, darling? You look a little worried."

"Maybe I am. After we met with Dr. Sharp last week, you said you didn't want to wait to try and have a baby. I took you at your word, but I just hope you aren't having reservations and afraid to tell me. If I haven't made you pregnant already, we could wait a while until you're absolutely sure."

She smiled. "I don't want to wait. Sometimes it takes a long time to get pregnant. Now that we're married, I don't want it to be an issue. One day I believe it will happen. If it's sooner, nothing could make me happier. I'm just so happy to be married to you. Whatever will be, will be."

He covered her face with kisses. "That works for me. Now I want to take a shower with you."

"I thought you'd never ask."

"I've been thinking about it for days." She hid her face in his neck. "I love the way you blush."

"Afterwards, I'll fix your breakfast."

"Let's do it together. I love doing everything with you, especially my therapy." He gently tilted her chin, forcing her to meet his gaze. "Tell me something, sweetheart. How many guys have you had to help the way you helped me? The truth now."

"A few, but they were simply a patient. You were different and you know it."

"You have no idea how hard it was when I had to go through the motions with Dr. Jensen. He didn't like me at all and I know why. The man was jealous of the time I spent with you."

"None of it matters."

"You're right. You're my wife and I'm the luckiest man alive." He rolled out of bed, then scooped her up in his arms. "How does that shower sound?"

"I can't wait."

Epilogue

Nine Months Later

Porter had just left for work when Lily felt a pain radiating from the base of her spine. It was the first she'd had at all during her whole pregnancy. She got up from the kitchen table and walked around for a few minutes to see if it would go away.

Both her mother and Millie, who'd recently had her baby, had told her what labor pains felt like. She was pretty sure this pain had nothing to do with going into labor. The doctor had kept a weekly check on her since April, but so far all had been well.

When a walk through the ranch house did nothing to alleviate it, she called the doctor and was told to come right in. After she hung up, she phoned Porter at headquarters. He'd arranged to work there for the last two months in case he needed to be around.

"I'm coming straight home."

By his grave-sounding voice, she knew he was alarmed. Lily was alarmed herself, but she had to remember what Dr. Sharp had told her during her first prenatal appointment. If her spine was in trouble because of the weight and location of the baby, they'd find out and do something about it fast.

While she waited, she called her mom to tell her what was happening.

"We'll be standing by and come if you need us."

"Thanks, Mom."

Lily hurried and put on her flowered-print smock top over her yellow maternity pants. Her feet were swollen, so she wore her white sandals. As her dad had told her yesterday, she looked in full bloom even though there was still a month to go.

"Lily?"

"Right here, darling. I'm coming."

He met her at the door. She hadn't seen lines in his face like that since the day he'd been wheeled into the therapy room the first time. "Are you still having those pains?"

"Yes. They haven't stopped."

"Let's go." He helped her to the car and they sped off to the doctor's office at the medical plaza.

Once they went inside, the doctor did a quick exam. Then she went back to his office where Porter was waiting. The doctor came in. "Someone from X-ray will come to get you. I want to find out what's going on with your spine."

"Can I go with her?"

"Certainly, Mr. Ewing."

The pain didn't get any worse, but it didn't get any better, either. Lily was glad when the X-rays had been taken. Porter wheeled her back to Dr. Sharp's office. He helped her into a chair and took the wheelchair out to the reception room, then came back.

Lily reached for his hand while they waited for her doctor. "I should be thankful I haven't had any pain until today."

He held his body taut. "You've been incredibly brave through this whole pregnancy. What's taking him so long?"

"I'm sure he's consulting with the radiologist and comparing the new X-rays to the old ones."

When she felt her husband couldn't stand the suspense any longer, Dr. Sharp came in. "I've made the decision that we'll take the baby out by cesarean section once you're admitted to the hospital. Take her over there now and get her admitted."

Porter's face lost color.

"I don't see any damage yet, but the pain isn't going to go away now. Having the baby will cure everything."

"Dr. Gregson said this could happen," she told her obstetrician.

"That's correct. And I like proceeding on the side of caution. Your baby boy will be four weeks premature, but he'll be fine. So will you. I'll see you over there shortly."

"Come on, sweetheart." Porter helped her out of the building to the car and drove her to the hospital. She called her parents to let them know what was happening.

Porter parked near the ER. "Home once again."

"Darling—everything really is going to be all right."

She heard his sharp intake of breath. "I know."

No, he didn't know and this was one time when she couldn't help him. "Just think. I don't have to go through labor like Millie and Jessica."

She couldn't get a smile out of him. He hurried around to help her inside. One of the nurses put her in a wheelchair and they were taken upstairs to a private room on the maternity ward.

While one nurse took Porter into an anteroom to put a surgical mask and gown on him, another nurse helped Lily into a hospital gown and got her into the bed where she'd have the baby.

Porter joined her. Then came someone to take her blood. Soon the anesthetist arrived to explain he was giving her an epidural. She lay on her side while he administered it.

He was followed by the neonatologist, who introduced himself and smiled.

"Are you two ready to have this baby?"

"I can't wait." Her voice shook.

Porter nodded, but she'd never seen him so frozen. Her poor darling husband was terrified. "Where's Dr. Sharp?"

"He's scrubbing and will be right in."

Lily was relieved when her doctor breezed in, gowned and masked. He sat down at the end.

"Porter? I want you to put that chair next to your wife's head. I'll need your help in a little while. Lily? I want you to relax and breathe deeply. This experience will be over before you know it. When I'm ready to pull the baby out, your anesthetist will give you some oxygen to breathe for just a minute or two. That's all you have to do."

"Okay."

She turned to look into Porter's eyes. "Our little boy's coming, darling."

"I can't believe it."

Neither could she.

The procedure really didn't take long. All of a sudden she heard the miraculous sound of a baby's cry. At that point the oxygen mask was put over her. She felt kind of odd, like her insides were all swooshing out of her. Then the mask was taken away.

"You've got a fine son here. Come over here, Porter. I'll let you cut the umbilical cord."

Lily watched as her husband did it perfectly. At that point the neonatologist took their crying baby over to a table, where he did an exam and cleaned him up. Then he stood up and brought him over to her, lying him on her chest.

"Congratulations, Mom and Dad. Your son weighed in at seven pounds, and is twenty-two inches. Not bad for being a month premature. His lungs are working beautifully. He's a perfect color and has all the right parts, in case you were worrying."

Porter let out a laugh, the first one she'd heard in days.

"What are you going to call him?"

"Rex, after my husband's father," Lily said, and saw Porter's eyes fill with tears.

"Go ahead, you two, and check him out," Dr. Sharp said. "Then he'll be taken to the nursery for a time. As for you, Lily, I don't anticipate you'll have any more pain because we removed the problem so fast. But we'll keep a close watch. I'll be back in later to check on you." Then he left.

"Oh, look at our little boy, darling. Isn't he adorable?"

Her husband examined him from head to toe. Then he looked at her with eyes that shone with a light she'd never seen before. "You two are the most beautiful sight I ever saw in my life. Are you all right, sweetheart?"

"I've never been better."

He furrowed his brow. "He doesn't have any hair yet."

"It'll come in. I wonder if it'll be black or blond?"

The baby started crying again. "I'm sure he's hungry."

The neonatologist lifted the baby and put him in a padded cart. "I'll take him to the nursery. You can come with me, Mr. Ewing. So can any family members."

After he left, Lily's mother and father came in. "We just saw the baby. He's the image of both of you. How are you feeling?"

"Incredibly happy, but tired."

"Of course you are."

"Come on, Porter," her father said. "Let's walk down to the nursery and have some fun."

He glanced at Lily. "I won't leave if you need me, darling."

"I'll always need you, but go with them for a few

minutes, then come back. We're a family now and this is just the beginning."

"My love," he half moaned the endearment with a kiss against her lips before leaving with her parents. She smiled and closed her eyes, imagining what their life was going to be like from now on. Absolutely wonderful!

* * * * *

When Matt looked up, she offered him a shy smile. "Like I said, I'm sorry. I should have told you that you were a father."

"You've got that right."

"I've made mistakes, but Emily isn't one of them. She's a great kid. So for now, let's focus on her."

"All right." Matt uncrossed his arms and raked a hand through his hair. "But just for the record, I would've done anything in my power to take care of you and Emily."

"I know." And that was why she'd walked away from him. Matt would have stood up to her father, challenged his threat, only to be knocked to his knees—and worse.

No, leaving town and cutting all ties with Matt was the only thing she could've done to protect him.

As she stood in the room where their daughter was conceived, as she studied the only man she'd ever loved, the memories crept up on her…the old feelings, too.

When she was sixteen, there'd been something about the fun-loving nineteen-year-old cowboy that had drawn her attention. And whatever it was continued to tug at her now. But she shook it off. Too many years had passed; too many tears had been shed.

Besides, an unwed single mother who was expecting another man's baby wouldn't stand a chance with a champion bull rider who had his choice of pretty cowgirls. And she'd best not forget that.

"Aw, hell," Matt said, as he ran a hand through his hair again and blew out a weary sigh. "Maybe you did Emily a favor by leaving when you did. Who knows what kind of father I would have made back then. Or even now."

Don't miss
The Cowboy's Secret Family *by Judy Duarte,*
available June 2019 wherever
Harlequin® Special Edition books and ebooks are sold.

www.Harlequin.com

Looking for more satisfying love stories with community and family at their core?

Check out **Harlequin®** **Special Edition** and **Love Inspired®** books!

 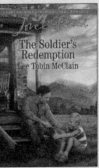

New books available every month!

CONNECT WITH US AT:

Facebook.com/groups/HarlequinConnection

 Facebook.com/HarlequinBooks

 Twitter.com/HarlequinBooks

 Instagram.com/HarlequinBooks

 Pinterest.com/HarlequinBooks

ReaderService.com

 HARLEQUIN®

ROMANCE WHEN YOU NEED IT